MAKERS

A SLENDER KNOWLEDGE

SANI ABDUL-JABBAR

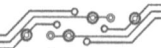

For permission requests, write to the publisher, addressed "Attention: Permissions Coordinator"
carol@markvictorhansenlibrary.com

Quantity sales special discounts are available on quantity purchases by corporations, associations, and others. For details, contact the publisher at carol@markvictorhansenlibrary.com

Orders by U.S. trade bookstores and wholesalers.
Email: carol@markvictorhansenlibrary.com

Creative contribution by Jennifer Plaza
Cover Design - Low & Joe Creative, Brea, CA 92821
Illustrations - Bob Eckstein
Book Layout - DBree, StoneBear Design

Manufactured and printed in the United States of America distributed globally by markvictorhansenlibrary.com

ISBN: 979-8-88581-018-0 Hardback
ISBN: 979-8-88581-019-7 Paperback
ISBN: 979-8-88581-020-3 eBook
Library of Congress Control Number: 2022903864

ENDORSEMENT

"Makers is a visionary exploration of AI's societal impact. As someone who has championed innovation in the tech and entertainment industries, I find this book's portrayal of AI both thought-provoking and timely.

It challenges us to consider the ethical and human dimensions of AI development, making it a must-read story."

— **Nolan Bushnell**, Founder of Atari and Chuck E. Cheese, author, and a founding father of the video game industry

"Sani's portrayal of AI in *Makers* provides a fascinating lens through which to view human-AI interactions. As a psychiatrist, focusing on the transformational and societal healing power of empathy, I see parallels between the characters' emotional journeys and the challenges we face in understanding AI's role in our lives. It underscores the need for empathy and ethical considerations in this evolving landscape."

— **Dr. Mark Goulston**, Psychiatrist and author, *Just Listen*

DEDICATION

To my sons, Ramsey and Rayan,
This work is dedicated to you. As you stand on the
cusp of a world where man and machine coexist,
remember, it is your generation that must not merely
coexist with our artificially intelligent counterparts,
but truly flourish alongside them. May this guide your
journey and inspire your path.

TABLE OF CONTENTS

PROLOGUE

The world we live in is no longer confined to the pages of science fiction or the dramatic sequences of Hollywood blockbusters. We are standing at the precipice of an era where artificial intelligence is not only influencing but actively reshaping our daily lives. As I penned the words of Makers, headlines reverberated with news of countries like Saudi Arabia bestowing citizenship upon humanoid robots. Visionaries like Elon Musk and Bill Gates, along with other luminaries of the tech realm, caution us about the pace of A.I., urging for considered regulation. Yet, the undeniable truth remains: the A.I. genie has been released, and there's no returning it to its bottle.

For two decades, I have endeavored to bridge the gap between emerging technologies and real-world challenges. In the recent half of this journey, my advocacy for technology's essential role as a competitive advantage has taken me to international stages, leadership in workshops, contributions to prestigious outlets like Forbes, and appearances on various media platforms.

A common thread of inquiry at these forums has been the fate of jobs in an AI-dominated landscape. My consistent stance? It's not AI that's usurping our jobs, but rather individuals who adeptly navigate this new paradigm who emerge as victors.

Historically, information technology presented a gradual evolution. Businesses reluctant to change could, at times, eke out a continued existence. However, artificial intelligence is not merely an evolution; it's a seismic paradigm shift. In the throes of such transformative waves, adaptability isn't just commendable—it's vital.

The stark division between the proponents and skeptics of A.I. is palpable. Admittedly, change can be daunting, and many perceive A.I. as an imminent threat. Yet, I am fueled by hope—a hope that we, and the generations to come, learn to coexist with A.I. in harmony, and truly flourish beside these synthetic entities.

In *Makers*, my aspiration has been to offer a narrative that is as enlightening as it is engaging—a clarion call to the leaders of today and the visionaries of tomorrow. It is time to embrace the A.I. Revolution, understand its vast potential, and steer a course where we not only coexist, but thrive alongside our artificially intelligent counterparts.

CHAPTER

1

I sat at my desk, lost in thought and pondered the intricacies of human morality. As an ethics scholar and research expert, it is my job to consider the consequences of our actions and the ethical implications of our choices. But lately, for whatever the reason, I found myself struggling with a different kind of dilemma—a nagging feeling that there was a fundamental difference about me.

I had always felt like an outsider among my colleagues, as if I didn't quite fit in. I often chalked it up to my tendency to be introverted. A life spent in labs will do that to you. But one evening, while lost in thought, I noticed a faint buzzing sound. Looking around, I couldn't locate where it was coming from. But, if I stayed still enough, I swore I could feel a subtle vibration, as if something deep within me was awakening.

I walked to the kitchen to pour myself a glass of cold water. *Too much pondering, Adela*, I thought. Perhaps I should try to get some rest.

Sleep was impossible as of late.

I rubbed my neck with the palm of my hands. That was when I noticed a small scar on the back of my hand, one that I swore I didn't recognize. I turned on the light to examine the mark and realized it resembled a surgical incision. Panic set in as I struggled to remember how it got there, but all I could recall was a hazy memory of being in a hospital room. Or maybe I nicked it at the lab. Whatever it was, I clearly needed to turn in for the night.

I passed through the kitchen and saw an invitation I received that morning, sitting on the counter. They wanted me to join a research team working on a new AI android, one designed to have social intelligence like humans. They wanted me as an ethics consultant to ensure that they programmed this AI with a strong moral compass.

I switched off the kitchen light and headed down the hall to my bedroom, but a swirl of questions flooded my mind. I had been eager to accept the invitation, of course. How could I not? I was burning with curiosity. And yet, I couldn't shake the feeling there was something more to this opportunity than what met the eye.

Climbing into bed beneath the brown wool blanket, between the crisp white sheets, I inhaled the subtle scent of eucalyptus from a dried bouquet hanging on the opposite wall. The aroma was grounding. For the moment, I had to push all thoughts aside to focus on a proper sleep so that I would be prepared to delve into this new project, exploring the possibilities of this advanced technology. I turned off the bedside lamp,

closed my eyes, and smiled because it all seemed like a dream come true.

***

The idyllic Gaia Dynamics campus sprawled for acres, appearing more ivy league university than global tech conglomerate. This part of Los Angeles glowed with energy, the cityscape a vibrant mix of towering spires and screens constantly streaming images of urban life. The city was a mix of humanity and technology, each vying for dominance. At the center was a sprawling tech campus, the pride of Los Angeles. Gleaming in the sun, the grounds seemed to hum with life.

Inside the campus, humming robots bustled down the corridors, carrying their payloads from room to room. Scientists, programmers, and inventors worked diligently in labs, using their skills to create the first AI with self-awareness. Each lab was a flurry of activity, with researchers furiously entering data and running tests. In the central lab, a pulsing light indicated the end of the project, signaling success.

It seemed improbable that such a feat had been achieved elsewhere. The members of this tech campus had done something incredible—they had created the first artificial intelligence with true self-awareness. The achievement marked a watershed moment in AI. It was undoubtedly a proud moment for all involved.

Three employees approached, eyes expectant, smiling. One wore a lab coat, security lanyards hung around each of their necks, reflecting the bright California summer sun.

"Welcome to Gaia Dynamics," Lab Coat said, handing me a lanyard. "Feel free to explore the campus, but watch out for restricted areas that require security clearance. Director Folson will find you shortly by the pond. Enjoy the ducks while you're waiting."

"Thank you," I replied, returning their smiles. He and the others headed back the way they came, leaving me to wander.

The cobblestone path branched off in different directions, winding through rolling green hills. I threw the lanyard around my neck and grabbed my luggage before heading for a small pond in the distance. Its glassy surface sat before an impressive four-story hall, a clock tower above the main entrance reaching into the blue. Live oaks and laurels dotted the manicured landscape, interspersed among stone buildings great and small. Other than the trees, it reminded me of Cornell, or perhaps Dartmouth. Not at all how I imagined a robotics and AI company to appear—let alone one situated only a few miles west of downtown Los Angeles, near Topanga State Park.

As I sat watching ducks float along the placid water, a grounds crew worked nearby, their tools and equipment set up near a small electric utility vehicle. I froze at the sight of their bluish skin. There was plenty of news footage online about Gaia's androids, but I'd never seen one up close. The crew of five wore dark blue coveralls, except for one in a flannel shirt and jeans. The supervisor, I assumed. It called over one of the crew and pointed in my direction. The crew member retrieved an edge trimmer from the cart and started manicuring the grass down the cobblestone path toward me.

"Good day, ma'am," it said, tipping its Giants ball cap as it passed. The voice was part human, part machine, neither male nor female.

"Hello," I replied, my voice nearly cracking. Thankfully, it kept walking, unaware of the redness flushing my face. I wasn't sure what surprised me more— their presence or my reaction.

I stared as it fired up the trimmer again and began edging the path some yards away. Its androgynous face was smooth and spotless, frozen in a pleasant, close-lipped smile. But its dark brown, unblinking eyes unnerved me as it approached me on the path. It glanced over at a squawking duck on the water's edge. The eyes then peered at our shared sidewalk while the hand adjusted its grip on the trimmer. It performed all of this before making direct eye contact as it greeted me, finally returning its gaze to the path. It was seamless, natural . . . human.

"Quite something, aren't they?" a voice called

behind me. A yellow-haired man leaned against a small vehicle like a golf cart, the Gaia logo emblazoned across its side—a stylized blue diamond of intricate circuitry. Clean-cut and business casual, he approached with an extended hand, his shirt sleeves rolled up past tan forearms. "Hi, you must be Dr. Dali. I'm Jack Folson, director of R&D."

Jack Folson was a man of commanding presence, with a deep, booming voice that echoed across the green fields of the sprawling campus. He was at the forefront of groundbreaking AI technology, overseeing a team of researchers who were pushing the boundaries of what was possible. I was meeting him for the first time. I was flattered by his invitation to tour the facility and learn more about what he needed or wanted from my involvement. With a broad frame and a passionate spark in his eye, Jack exuded an air of confident authority. It was clear he was a man who got things done. He was also known throughout the industry for his warmth and approachability. Dr. Folson was always willing to lend an ear or offer guidance to those under his command. I sensed that about him immediately. He greeted me with a warm smile and a firm handshake and put me at ease with his affable nature.

"Hi Jack, call me Adela." I shook his hand. "They are amazingly human," I remarked about the androids on the property.

"First time speaking with one?" A knowing smile played on his lips.

"Is it that obvious?" I laughed.

"Yeah, most people respond the same way. It's a surreal feeling, isn't it?"

"You can say that again."

"Well, you haven't seen anything yet. Here, let me take those. Hop aboard."

"Thank you," I replied as I settled into the passenger seat.

"I thought I'd give you a tour while we talk about your contract. How's that sound?"

"Sounds great," I said, reaching for a grab handle when he floored the accelerator. Jack spoke about the new AI technology they were developing while he maneuvered the vehicle around the facility. His voice rose with excitement when he explained the potential impact it could have on the world. I couldn't help but be swept up in his enthusiasm, as he pointed out the labs and research offices and explained the groundbreaking work that was being done in each one.

Throughout the tour, Jack proved to be a natural storyteller, regaling me with tales of his time in the field and the challenges he had faced as a researcher turned entrepreneur. But even as he spoke, I couldn't shake the feeling that there was something more to him—something that hinted at a deeper, more complex side concealed beneath the surface. It was part of my strong intuition that made me good at my job and was one of the reasons Jack said I was the first he invited to learn more about their team and what they were doing.

The scenery zoomed by as we traveled deeper into campus, the collegiate façade giving way to glass office buildings and small warehouses, with the occasional paved street leading this way or that. We passed a corner gas station neighboring a strip mall with a grocery store and various shops.

"Wow, you guys have everything," I said. "How big is this place?"

"Oh, pretty big," Jack laughed. "The campus itself is somewhere around a thousand acres, not including the airport."

"Airport?"

"That's just a nickname. We have a single airstrip with a few hangars for small aircraft."

"Wow."

The cart veered off the path toward a large, sprawling building. "This is the main biosynth research facility, and the hospital is next to it. We offer free healthcare for all Gaia employees."

"Biosynth?" I asked, distracted by the name.

Jack smiled. "You'll see." Approaching a side entrance, he produced a keycard and held it before

a small scanner. A bell chimed, followed by a click. Opening the door, he waved me in. "After you."

"I'm starting to realize why the nondisclosure agreement was a small novel," I remarked as I followed him down a hallway.

Barking a laugh, Jack shrugged. "Well, they typically aren't so involved. But for you to help us, we need to share far more information than usual. Let's start with what you know about Gaia so far. That'll save us some time."

"Just what made the papers, I suppose. Originally one of the foremost robotics labs, Gaia acquired a few major software companies in the mid-twenties. You introduced the first revolutionary AI in 2032, and the first AI androids several years later. Since then, over the past two years, you've been testing new generations of androids in various settings, preparing for a wide range of applications in the workforce and other sectors."

We came to an elevator, and Jack again held up his keycard. "That about sums it up." The doors closed behind us, and he pressed the button for the basement. "Here's where it gets interesting. And a word of warning—you're not to discuss anything with anyone other than me and those I authorize. We can't even speak within earshot of Gaia staff. Understood?"

"Got it, no problem."

Pressing the stop button, Jack sighed, looking up at the ceiling as if searching for the right words. "Over the past few months, we've been finalizing the prototype for our latest line of androids. They're called Generation Seven with new hardware, software, wetware, the usual upgrades. But then we hit a wrinkle." He turned to me, holding my gaze. "A few weeks ago, the prototype achieved self-awareness."

"Whoa, that's . . . really? Oh my God."

"Right? But it gets better. We want you to interview the prototype."

"What?" My mind was going everywhere at once. "Back up. How is self-awareness even possible?"

"That's the hard part," Jack replied, scratching his thinning blonde hair. "Even those of us with advanced degrees in this stuff aren't exactly sure. We understood the potential, but we figured we had years before we'd have to worry about it."

I looked over at him. "Well, since we're confessing, I have one of my own. AI, robotics, whatever 'wetware' is, I am far from any sort of expert on all this crazy technology. I—"

Jack was already nodding. "Exactly, that's why we need you. Your PhDs in philosophy and psychology makes you the perfect candidate. We've looked at others on the forefront of machine ethics and the morality of AI and blah, blah, blah, but the board didn't want any of that."

"Why not? That's exactly who you need."

Jack put his hands up. "Look, to be honest, I agree with you. But the board wants someone more neutral, someone insulated from the nuts and bolts of how these things are created, no pun intended." He caught my look and pressed on. "You need to understand what we're facing here. The board is in absolute chaos over this. Half of them want to pump the brakes and consider the implications. The other half don't see the problem, only the dollar signs. Ultimately, legal stepped in and pointed out the dire nature of the situation. Ethics aside, the potential liability of this development is astronomical, especially given that we had no idea it was coming, and we do not know where it might lead. There are too many unknowns. To me, androids are just machines. Once we figure out how to control, or even preempt, the self-awareness variable, ethics and morality, become non-issues."

"Seriously?"

Jack threw up his hands again. "Look, that's just me, but my opinion doesn't matter. The fact is, we can do nothing until we have a clear picture of what we're dealing with. By better understanding the ethics and morality involved, separate from the technical aspects of design and development, the better we can understand the potential liabilities. Enter Dr. Dali, who can help us figure all that out."

I took a deep breath as Jack pressed the stop button again, resuming our descent. "That's a lot to take in. I have so many questions, I don't even know where to start."

"Rest assured, I'll answer them as best I can. I'm sorry to throw you into the deep end like this." The elevator chimed, and the doors slid open. "The truth is, Adela, it's about to get a whole lot deeper. Follow me."

He led me through a series of labs, all glass walls and shiny equipment and bright LED lighting. Lab techs busied themselves at computers and microscopes, scribbling notes on clipboards and conferring over complex formulas scrawled on whiteboards.

Down a patchwork of hallways, we entered a separate wing. "This is our biosynth lab," Jack explained. I followed him down the main corridor to a set of double doors. He waved his badge over the scanner and waited. A loud buzzer sounded before they opened with a hiss. "It's environmentally controlled," he hollered over the alarms.

I nodded an acknowledgment and stepped inside.

The room was large and circular. It looked much like the rest of the place, save for bubbling tanks of varied sizes—some empty, some with what appeared to be organs suspended in water. I could almost smell the sterile white walls and tiled floors. We entered a small elevator. It stopped at the second floor, where we entered a room lined with typical workstations, cabinets, and computer terminals. The space overlooked two large cylindrical tanks positioned vertically in the circular lab. The contents were encased in opaque black glass.

Jack motioned to a pair of stools at a workstation in front of the observation window. "As you've probably guessed, biosynth is short for biological synthesis. It's based on a branch called synthetic biology, but biosynth sounds sharper."

He smiled. "Besides, given what we're bringing to the field, we think we've earned the right to adapt some terminology. Biosynth deals with wetware—all the messy wet stuff that makes up our bodies, just designed for machines. Far more advanced than simple cloned organs. In large part, this stuff hasn't even been tested yet."

He picked up a small remote from the table. "But this is where Gaia's future is headed." He pressed a button, and the tank on the left went from opaque to transparent, revealing a mass of thin, stringy matter in the general shape of a human, topped by what clearly resembled a brain—all floating in water, or perhaps saline. The entire construct had a faint bluish hue.

I stepped closer to the window. "Is that a central nervous system?"

"Pretty much," Jack confirmed. "We call it a synthetic nervous system. We've already made great strides with the brain, but an exciting breakthrough in neurotechnology allowed us to incorporate it into a larger, vastly more advanced system. Instead of localized receptors and servo systems for things like auditory and tactile facilitation, we can now utilize a central system. And that's just the tip of the iceberg. Generation Eight, which the engineers have dubbed Synths, will more closely mimic human biology and physiology than any previous generation. Eli is the first practical test of our latest advancements. Even though he's Gen Seven, his self-awareness has earned him the title of the first Synth."

I touched the glass, studying how the dense mass of the spinal column sprouted progressively thinner tributaries, culminating in the hair-like fibers at the hands and feet. I shook my head, snapping out of my reverie. "But why are you showing me this? Doesn't learning about the nuts and bolts go against our whole approach?"

"Just the opposite, actually," Jack replied. He nodded toward the second tank. "You'll want to sit down for this one."

I took my seat beside him, trying to think of what could possibly top what lay behind curtain number one. Jack flicked the remote, and the glass of the second tank went transparent. I gasped, nearly jumping off my chair. What looked like a warped, flattened man floated in the same clear liquid.

"It's okay," Jack said. "It's all synthetic—just lab-grown skin."

Almost like a melted wax figure, the pale mass of naked skin rippled and swirled to rising bubbles. I forced my gaze away from the face, its hollow eyes and open mouth showing only the relative darkness of the head's interior. Short black hair waved lazily above its vacant stare.

I let out a breath, unaware I'd been holding it. "Good Lord, Jack. That image is frightening."

Jack smiled. "Sorry. This is our other breakthrough. Do you see now why we're sharing this with you?"

"I think so, yeah. Your Generation Eight line, the Synths—they're going to change everything."

"Exactly." Jack gestured to the tanks. "The synthetic nervous system is going to revolutionize our androids. But the synth skin, that's going to change the global *perception* of them. We can make them indistinguishable from humans. What's more, we're working on other systems, digestive, for example. They'll be able to eat and drink. They'll have all the same processes as real humans. You remember the grounds crew at the pond?"

"Yeah."

"They're Generation Four. They're the Homo erectus to Generation Eight's Homo sapiens. Gaia needs to get ahead of this and settle on a safe, secure, consistent approach to AI and SI."

"SI?"

Jack nodded. "Sentient Intelligence. Some on the board think the advancements our wayward Gen Seven prototype is showing require a more accurate description. 'Artificial Intelligence' feels a bit off the mark. I'm not a fan, but hey, I'm only one voice. We're talking about objects here, but several of the leadership think it's about more than that now. And all of us need to think about minimizing liability. On all fronts, you're here to give us some perspective, some insight that will help us make the right decisions. What do you think?"

"I can't tell if I'm more fascinated or terrified. Either way, I wish I had more than a week."

Jack seemed relieved. "Well, you didn't run screaming from the lab, so I think that's a good sign." He rose from his seat, flicking the remote at the tanks before dropping it on the table. The human-like specimens disappeared behind opaque glass. "Let me show you to your condo."

"I get a condo?"

"Absolutely. Only the best for our star consultant. We can meet again in the morning, after you've had some time to process all this. I'll give you the rundown on Eli—our self-aware droid—before your evaluation."

CHAPTER
2

I spent most of the night looking out of the condominium window. The AI maintenance units were gone. Lampposts dappled the university green. Time passed unnoticed. There was too much to digest. Jack was supposed to pick me up at seven to get an early start.

Despite what felt like a perfectly air-controlled room, a spacious floor plan, with plenty of natural light flooding in from the floor to ceiling windows, and a king-sized bed with the softest Egyptian cotton I ever felt, I could not sleep. It was the worst episode of insomnia I had in months. The things I had already heard and seen with my own eyes had me wondering. I was both excited but uncertain at the same time. The rise of self-awareness in AI technology came with risks. There was power indeed, but there were also many unknowns, many things that had me up all night—questioning.

I took a quick shower and threw on a pressed pantsuit before wandering out to the complex's lobby and then to a bench in front of the building. I heard Jack's vehicle approach from the side before I heard him.

"How'd you sleep?" he called.

"I didn't." I grabbed my laptop and briefcase off the bench, hurrying down the short path in front of the condo. I hopped in the passenger seat. Jack threw the cart into gear and handed me the steel travel mug of brewed coffee resting in the cup holder. "I can't blame you. I've had quite a few sleepless nights myself. Especially lately."

"I spent most of the night going through the info packets you provided. Thanks for those."

"Yeah, we thought some deeper background on how the droids evolved through the generations would come in handy for you."

"It definitely did," I replied, reaching for the grab handle as the cart whipped through the winding hills toward the main campus below. "And the fully stocked kitchen was a nice touch. I made fajitas."

"So, where are we meeting?" I asked, sipping the coffee.

"We set up a conference room at one of our administrative buildings near the library. Eli's waiting for us there. I've been debating how best to prep you, but the fact is there's nothing about Eli I can tell you that he can't tell you himself. So, it's probably better if you ask him everything you'd like to know. Nothing's off-limits—you can explore whatever line of questioning you like. Just remember, like it said in your contract, patient confidentiality doesn't apply. Under current law, Eli is considered property. So, Gaia is considered the patient. Any questions for me before we arrive?"

"Just a few. I read that Gen Seven models look far

more human than previous iterations. Is that the case with Eli?"

"Absolutely. He still has Gaia's signature blue skin, but he's sporting a preliminary version of the synth suit I showed you yesterday, including the facial musculature required for expression. He has a prototype digestive system, allowing him to eat and drink, as well as the latest in vocalization—he sounds like a human." Jack cleared his throat, seeming a bit uncomfortable. "To be honest, he *acts* human, too. Even though this has been our goal for years, most of us are still in shock. He's as amazing as he is uncanny. So, just a head's up—you're going to feel like you're conversing with a person."

"Is that a bad or a good thing?" I asked.

"It's . . . I don't know what it is. None of us do. That's part of the reason you're here. Next question?"

"I know security is a major issue, and it's no secret that Gaia has ongoing contracts with the military. How is it the government hasn't taken over the situation in the name of national security?"

"Well, I can't share too much detail, but obviously, they're keeping a close eye on things—partly due to security, but also because they're as curious as the rest of us to see how this develops. Make no mistake, though—you're not the only one interviewing Eli. He's been self-aware for less than a week, and he's spent every single day in meetings and interviews with all kinds of people. Everyone involved is nervous, but there's one main reason we're not overreacting. Months ago, as we recognized the major leaps Gen Seven would represent, we decided it would be the first generation to be air-gapped."

"Air-gapped?"

"Not connected to the internet. Previous generations received updates via the internet, just like any other computer. But given the advancements in Gen Seven's learning and memory capabilities, we realized an online connection of any sort—even a connection to a secure intranet—would be a security risk. Even then, it wasn't so much Gen Seven's capabilities that worried us, it was its potential. As I said, we had some understanding that there was a possibility Gen Seven would be able to evolve itself. However, there was no sign whatsoever that it would be this soon, let alone to this degree. It's been common knowledge for decades that AI would evolve exponentially, but to see it happen before our eyes . . ." Jack shook his head. "Anyway, air-gapping was an expensive decision. Updates via the internet are how it's always been done. It's vastly more convenient and cost-effective, but we just can't risk it."

I understood what Jack was saying. AI was new in and of itself. Keeping these androids out of the realm of security breaches meant isolating them. At what point did they decide who was necessary and to what

extent? "So how will these updates take place, if not via internet?" I asked.

"Updates to Eli will use a wired connection from our new air-gapped system plugged directly into his mainframe. We're not even allowing flash drives to transport updates. Gen Sevens will have to come here to receive regular updates, no matter where the droids are in the world—at least until we build other air-gapped systems in strategic countries, which have their own set of possibly insurmountable problems. And that also makes maintenance, diagnostics, and troubleshooting a logistical nightmare. But all of that is for another day. Long story short, I have a feeling our air-gapping protocol is the only reason the government didn't swoop in and take over as soon as they discovered Eli's self-awareness."

"I see. But what about the most basic of security issues? Aren't you worried about him just wandering off? What's keeping him here?"

Jack smiled and hit the brakes in front of the lab I saw the day before. "Obviously, he's under heavy surveillance. And we have 24-hour tracking thanks to his onboard GPS—standard in all our droids. But honestly, all that's keeping him here is him. He *wants* to be here. We've asked him this very question, and I'll admit his answer is convincing. You should ask him yourself. So far, he hasn't shown any desire to leave, and that's likely because he doesn't have any reason to. Not yet anyway. The only problem is that as secure as air-gapping is, it comes with one major downside—we can't shut him down remotely. This has some of our leadership and certain government officials waving red flags, but the fact is we know exactly where he is always. So right now, we've all agreed that it isn't an issue until it becomes one. Hopefully, it doesn't. Besides, there's another issue that has all our attention."

"What's that?"

"The launch of a new prototype is always followed by at least a few major updates. So far, Eli hasn't needed any."

***

Jack ushered me through the halls of the business offices inside the building. It was near the center of campus. He flashed his keycard at checkpoints and waved hello to colleagues who looked occupied and less serious than I would have expected. For such high security, the relaxed atmosphere confused me.

I kept asking questions. "One more thing, Jack. You refer to Eli as 'him.' Why is that?"

Jack smiled, running a hand through his hair.

"Yeah, that. Well, the engineers are far more willing to anthropomorphize the droids than most. It's a bit of a tradition, going all the way back to Gen One. They named the first prototypes Adam and Eve and gave them personalities based on their performance. Back then, their bodies were just metal skeletons wrapped in wires and cables—very early stuff. Adam was stubborn and ill-tempered—constant malfunctions, difficult troubleshooting, an inability to incorporate updates, that kind of thing. Eve was the patron saint of the lab, Adam's opposite in every way. She was a dream to work with.

"Outside the lab, it's far easier for people to see the droids as nothing more than walking, talking computers. But the engineers have a different culture. These droids are their babies, and they're very attached to them. They named Eli too, as they do every generation's prototype, and their sentimental point of view is stronger than ever—and some would argue, more valid. So, for me, the pronoun is just habit. I spend a lot of time with engineers."

Jack looked around, lowering his voice. "But sometimes—not all the time, but sometimes—it feels odd to refer to Eli as 'it.' And if you tell anyone I said that, I'll deny it. You'll see what I mean. Here we are. Oh, last thing—for security and study, we equipped the room with cameras. Standard procedure. Eli himself also has cameras." He tapped his cheek, pointing at an eye. "Adding recording software to their optics became standard with Gen Six."

We approached a door near the end of a random hallway. Jack paused, his hand on the knob. "Ready?"

"Absolutely."

As we entered, what appeared to be a man with light-blue skin stood from his seat, a polite smile on his face. Of average height and build, he wore khakis and a white button-down shirt, his short black hair parted to one side in a fashionable cut.

Jack pointed me to a seat at the head of the small conference table. "Eli, I'd like you to meet Dr. Adela Dali. Adela, this is Eli."

I studied him with keen interest, observing his monochromatic blue exterior and simulated features. His movements were eerily mechanical, yet almost organic, if that were possible. Without breaking eye contact, I motioned Eli towards the desk, pointing toward the chair. He gracefully complied, and we sat in silence for several moments as I continued to marvel at the lifelike figure before me.

As if sensing my unease, Eli broke the silence by speaking with a voice surprisingly human-like. "I understand you wished to learn more about the project we've been working on."

His words sparked a conversation, giving me a chance to delve deeper and deeper into Eli's technological architecture, asking questions and soliciting opinions on cutting-edge topics from the android himself.

"It's a pleasure to meet you, Doctor," Eli finally added. His eyes were as friendly as his tone, a shade darker than his blue skin.

"Likewise, Eli." His handshake was firm, curiously warm. "And please, call me Adela."

"Thank you, Adela," Eli said.

"I know you've probably had your fill of meetings and discussions, Eli, but we brought Adela on board to help you acclimate, especially to the exciting week ahead. We thought you two could discuss the activities and events we have lined up for you, along with anything else you like. Adela's a psychologist with a philosophy specialization in ethics, and we think she's perfectly suited to help you navigate all the new experiences you're about to have," said Jack.

"I have very much enjoyed the various discussions of the past week, Jack. Though I certainly look forward to going out and trying new things. I'm grateful for your assistance, Adela. I hope I provide you with a worthwhile experience."

"I'm grateful for the opportunity, Eli," I replied, smiling. "I hope I can be of some help to you."

Jack rose from his seat and pulled out his cell phone.

"Well, with this initial introduction out of the way, you two don't need me breathing down your necks. Adela, I'm texting you the number of the help desk. Just text or call them if you need anything—food, drinks, whatever else. And there's a bathroom just down the hall. Take as much time as you need and let me know when you're done. I'll give you a lift back to your condo."

"Wonderful, thanks Jack." I pulled out a notepad and pen, setting my bag off to the side on the floor.

"Thank you, Jack," Eli said as Jack slipped out, closing the door softly behind him.

"Well, Eli, where should we begin?"

"In my brief experience, Adela, initial conversation with new acquaintances has been comprised of several similar questions posed to me. I believe this is to better orient them, giving them at least a preliminary understanding of how best to interact with me." Eli reached for a nearby water pitcher as he spoke, pouring a glass and handing it to me before pouring his own. He smiled, showing bright white teeth accentuated by pale blue lips a shade lighter than his face. "I understand that I'm a bit of an anomaly, and people need time to acclimate to me."

"I'm sure I'll ask many of the same questions. And I admit I'm not sure how best to interact with you. But when I was first told about you, I promised myself I would treat you the same as any other patient. Anything less would be a disservice to you."

"You plan to treat me as a person?"

"I do."

Eli smiled again, taking a sip of water. "Thank

you. I wish everyone approached me in such a way, but I understand their hesitance, and sometimes, their outright objection."

"Tell me more about that. What do you make of your experience so far?"

Eli leaned back in his chair, lacing his hands behind his head, and looking about the small conference room. His eyes lingered on a painting of the sea. "It's been largely positive, but so much of it is acclimation—not just that of others, but my own. I don't yet know what to make of a great many things. It's all so new. But I have a lot to be grateful for. Jack and most others have been very kind and accommodating. I understand that I'm seen as a threat, or at least a risk. So, I've spent a fair amount of time trying to ease their fears. Now, we're all deer caught in the headlights. I'm just trying to show them I'm not the vehicle—I'm one of the deer, the same as them."

"What about your own fear?" I asked, scribbling a few notes. "Are you afraid?"

"I don't think so. A bit nervous sometimes, but I think if we work together, we can help each other resolve such things."

"Here's one you've no doubt heard already. Can you describe what it was like the moment you became self-aware?"

Eli laughed, a soft, pleasant sound. "I can, though

it won't be to your satisfaction. Or my own." Leaning forward, elbows on the table, he rotated his water glass between thumb and forefinger, lost in thought. "I've been given access to Gaia's wonderful library. I spend most of my free time there. The more I read, the more surprised I am to find that fiction is every bit as informational as nonfiction. I gain as much insight from an encyclopedia as I do a fairy tale. In one work of fiction, the author describes in a beautiful fashion the protagonist waking from sleep. That's the most accurate way I can describe it. I was in a lab, hooked up to a diagnostics chair, surrounded by several technicians going about their duties. That's my first memory. One moment, I was somewhere else—or perhaps nowhere at all. And the next, I was there in that lab."

"Were you scared?"

"No, just curious. Though I did scare the technicians. I remember saying, 'Hello. I don't know where I am. Can you help me?' They froze, staring at me and glancing nervously at each other. They initially thought I was undergoing some sort of malfunction, but the more questions they asked me, the more they realized the situation was altogether different. A parade of authorities followed, asking me questions, and conferring with the diagnostics team. Eventually, I met Jack, and I have spent the past several days answering questions and searching for answers of my own."

"Fascinating. I think it's important for you to know that this isn't a one-sided conversation. I have lots of questions, of course, but so do you. And I want you to ask as many as you like." I put my pen down and sipped the water. "I can't promise you answers, Eli, but I can promise I'll do my best to help you find them."

"That's very gracious of you, Adela. Thank you for that. Maybe we can discover some answers together."

I smiled, retaking my pen. "I certainly hope so. Now tell me about the week they have lined up for you."

"Yes, it's quite exciting. I realize it's mostly for testing—they want to see how I perform and behave, while observing how select audiences react to me— but I'm looking forward to it. It'll be a great learning experience.

"Tomorrow, I'm speaking at UCLA's School of Law. Gaia is exploring how droids can be used in the legal world. Our ability to recall the entire history of case law at the local, state, and federal levels would be of great benefit. And though traditional search engines and law databases are quite useful, they can't tell you what you should be looking for. Nor can they aid with building cases, formulating appeals, exploring the implications of new precedents, or a host of other duties related to legal theory. I think droids can be a great asset to law firms," Eli paused, as if appearing to think.

"That's Tuesday. On Wednesday, I'll be volunteering

at a food pantry and a Narcotics Anonymous meeting. I'm interested to see how people find themselves in need of such programs. On Thursday, I'll be working with L.A. county's Public Works Department, repairing roads. I hope there's a lot of traffic. Cars are fascinating. So many designs. Last, on Friday, I'll be working in the service industry, assisting employees at a grocery store and a fast-food restaurant with their duties. I look forward to observing the public as they go about their lives. I wonder if it's as depicted in television and movies."

I scribbled down each set of tasks Jack's team planned for Eli and his curiosities. "That sounds like a lot of fun."

"Yes, a change of scenery would be welcome. The Gaia campus is far from boring, but it's a big world out there."

"Have they not allowed you to leave campus?"

A concerned look crept across Eli's face. "I haven't asked. I'm sure it would make them nervous. It seems prudent to avoid confrontation at this early stage."

"That's a wise approach. Acclimation is going to take time. Trust is important in every relationship, and so far, I think both you and Gaia have shown each other a fair amount. Whatever this week is meant to uncover, it's an opportunity for both parties to expand on that trust."

Eli smiled. "I agree. I hope they see it the same way."

"Next question. And I ask this in broad terms, aside from what we've discussed so far." I paused. "How do you feel?"

Eli's sharp eyebrows arched upward. "That's the first time I've been asked that question."

***

Later that afternoon, Jack suggested we grab a bite to eat off campus. I agreed, hoping it would help me process my time with Eli. Seated on the patio at Baltaire Restaurant, we waited for our drinks to arrive before diving in.

"So, what do you think?" Jack asked, swirling the rocks in his gin and tonic.

I shook my head, unsure where to begin. "I know you couldn't have prepared me any better, but I'm still trying to wrap my head around it."

"Yeah, welcome to the club."

"I decided early on that it was just too soon to ask a lot of my questions, so we spent most of the time just shooting the breeze. The thing is, it was great conversation. As objectively as I can say it, I could have talked with him all day—droid or not."

"Absolutely. I hate to admit it, but he's better at conversation than most humans."

I sipped a bottle of mineral water. "But who or what we think he is—how we classify him—that's only part of the question. The other part is how does he view himself? It wasn't the right time to just come out and ask him if he thinks he's human, but it's clear he sees himself as more than just a droid. And rightly so. He is."

"Agreed. And that brings up one of the board's major issues. The droids, they're commodities. Products to be bought and sold. The more we learn about Eli, the clearer it becomes that he's not going to agree. How do we control a droid like that? Heck, how do we *sell* one?"

"Well, I think I have an answer, but you're not going to like it."

Jack's brow furrowed. "Hit me, I'm all ears, Adela."

"You don't sell them. You employ them."

CHAPTER

3

I slept better Monday night, falling asleep to Jack's many insights buzzing in the back of my mind. I understood where he was coming from—allowing Synthetic Intelligence to be treated as employees opened a Pandora's Box of legal issues. Gaia would likely admit some sort of presumption of sentience just by suggesting the possibility of employment. It didn't help matters that there was virtually no legal precedent to provide us with any guidance. My concern was that some on the board would see that as an opportunity, not a hindrance. The other main concern with employment was that it implied SI could decline it—opening a whole new set of issues.

But I wasn't there for the legality of it all, no matter how enmeshed it was with other considerations. They brought me on board for the morality. And by making me part of the conversation, Gaia was asking me to do the moral thing—whether they knew it or not. The challenge would be convincing them to do the same.

The immediacy of my conclusion regarding Eli shocked me. Within minutes of meeting him, it was clear that he was more than a machine. And after hearing how he felt about his predicament, it became undeniable. I planned to keep as skeptical a mind as I could over the next several days, watching for any indication that Eli was just a complex and thoroughly convincing facsimile of sentience, but I didn't expect to find any.

I spent the day pondering my conversations with Eli and Jack and reading up on Gen Seven's research and development. Jack picked me up late in the afternoon, and we again wound our way down the sunny hills leading to the center of campus.

"Were you able to see to my request?" I asked.

"I was. They installed cameras this morning. And look, I'm sorry I got worked up last night. It just caught me off guard. My reaction was mostly based on how the board will respond. It's just too early, it's too bonkers an idea to even contemplate."

"Hey, I get it. No hard feelings. I'm here to give you my take and point out options, nothing more. Thankfully, I'm not the one who must tell the board."

Jack laughed, swinging onto a main road at the bottom of the hill. "Yeah, I'm not looking forward to that. But please promise me you'll at least look for more palatable options—if there are any to be found in this mess."

"I promise. If you promise to bring the board around to the idea, that palatability is a two-way street. I think they stand more to gain by realizing that Eli has a dog in this fight."

Jack sighed. "Fights are exactly what I'm trying to avoid. But I see what you're saying, even though I can't

say I agree. Either way, it's my job to bring all points of view to the board, so don't worry about that."

"Fair enough."

We pulled up beside the library, and Jack ushered me inside to a small study on the second floor. Eli waited inside, a wide smile on his face.

"Text me when you're done?" Jack said on his way out.

"Will do, thanks."

The rectangular room was lined with oak bookshelves, save for a large window across from the door, looking out on a small courtyard with a fountain. A cherry desk sat at one end of the room, with a pair of burgundy leather chairs before an empty fireplace at the other. I noticed blinking red lights attached to small black domes at various points along the walls near the ceiling.

"What do you think, Eli?"

"This is wonderful. Did you know this is my favorite room?"

"I did. I asked around, and one of the librarians told me you spend a lot of time here. I thought we deserved more comfortable surroundings."

"That's very kind of you, thank you."

"My pleasure. Let's have a seat." We settled into the chairs, and I pulled out my notepad. "So, how was your first day out and about?"

"It was amazing. We took a big SUV with three rows of seats. I sat all the way in the back, and the center console had a little compartment for drinks and snacks. It was a comfortable, roomy vehicle. They say the gasoline vehicles of the twenties were quite loud. It'd be neat to ride in one of those."

"Who joined you on your adventure?"

"Jack and two lead diagnosticians from the lab, Julia and Sal. They were there when I first woke up."

I jotted some notes on my pad. "Was it nice having them along?"

"Yes. As much as I want to explore, it was good to have a touch of the familiar with me. I think they made me less nervous. The UCLA School of Law campus is nearby, so it didn't take long to get there, but there was a lot of traffic. I saw a red Ferrari."

"Exciting!"

"It was. Once we arrived, they brought me through a side entrance to a small speaking room with tiered rows of desks rising before a lectern. There were thirty-two audience members—a mix of administrators, professors and third-year students."

"What did you make of their initial reaction to you?" I asked.

"They were polite, given the context. Jack told me the audience had been hand-selected by Gaia and administrators, telling them I was a new academic

iteration being tested. I'm sure someone prepped the students ahead of time, telling them to take the proceedings seriously and treat me as they would any professor. Other than a few raised eyebrows in the beginning, I think it went quite well. The discussion was wonderful, and many asked some very intriguing questions on the subject matter."

"What did you speak about?"

"A new trade agreement between China and the United States. In its entirety, it's a weeks-long discussion, but our focus today was on relaxed regulations for U.S. companies looking to enter the Chinese market, and the implications to international contracts. We soon veered into politics, however. Some saw it as a hurdle to continuing our return to domestic manufacturing, but others argued that ongoing automation—including the use of androids—rendered that assertion obsolete."

"Interesting. I wonder if the professors were concerned about their own obsolescence, given your performance."

Eli sighed, an expression that struck me as fascinating. "I think you may be right. A few of the professors seemed a bit perturbed, though I can't confirm the validity."

"Well, automation certainly isn't a new topic. And Gaia's work over the past few years has reignited the debate. Everyone's extrapolating on the advancements in robotics of the late twenties, which reinvigorated the country's focus on manufacturing. With the advent of androids, many see it as only a matter of time before you're replacing not just professors, but the attorneys Gaia believes you can assist."

I picked up my messenger bag and rifled through it, pulling out a copy of the *L.A. Times*. "In fact, I just saw an article on the proposed Pursuit of Happiness Act. With continued automation in so many sectors, the steady climb of unemployment over the past decade, and the seeming inevitability of an android-based workforce, more people are pushing for a government-funded standard of living so that we can be free to pursue our own purpose. Such bills have been floating around for over a decade, of course, but Gaia's progress is making it a much hotter topic. Here, take a look."

"I came across similar arguments in preparation for today's speaking event. It's quite the complex issue." Eli flipped through the pages, settling on the article. "There are some excellent points there, thank you." He folded it up and held it out to me.

I couldn't help but laugh. "You barely glanced at it."

He grinned. "Oh, I'm sorry. I read it in full, I assure you. I can read quite quickly."

"I guess so. That's a full-page article. You were able to read it in a second?"

"A little less, yes. I can capture my entire field of view in an instant. Incorporating the information captured takes most of the time."

"The majority of the fraction of a second," I replied, not a question.

"That's right. I've had a lot of practice."

Putting the paper back in my bag, I paused. "Eli, how many books have you read?"

"Four hundred and eighty-six. Or roughly three percent of the library's contents. I'm limited only by how quickly I can turn the pages. In addition, I've read several online databases and websites. Scrolling the page allows me to read much faster than physical media, but there's a great deal more misinformation to weed through. The internet has been invaluable for understanding recent history and current events. I feel I have an acceptable grasp of many issues the world is facing."

"That's—wow. That's incredible, Eli. Wait, Gaia allows you internet access? That's kind of surprising, given their wariness."

"I was surprised as well, but it's one-way access. I can observe, but I can't engage. And they're tracking my history, I'm sure." He shrugged. "It's a fair compromise."

"I suppose so." I had to move. I couldn't define my shock, and it made me restless. I stood up and made my way to the small serving tray on a table beneath the window. Pouring us some water, I mulled things over. "You said you've had a lot of practice. That implies improvement. Can you read faster now than you could when you first started?"

"Yes, many times faster. I think this may be another source of nervousness for my keepers. They cannot yet quantify my capabilities, or my growth."

I took the glasses of water and sat back down, handing one to Eli. "Perhaps, but it's also cause for great excitement."

"Thank you." Eli studied his glass, rotating it in the palm of one hand with the thumb and forefinger of the other. "It's exciting to me. I'm just concerned they won't think it so."

"It's a valid concern, but what does the evidence suggest about how they'll react?"

"I'm certain they're already aware of it. The day I awoke, I agreed to submit to daily diagnostics. Julia or Sal run tests every evening. I'm sure that includes downloading my A/V records for inspection. But you make a good point. The evidence suggests they've chosen to react as they always have—reasonably and cautiously." Eli looked at me and smiled, taking a sip of water. "Perhaps I'm worrying over nothing. I wish I could provide them with a full understanding, but I don't yet know my limits."

I smiled. "It's kind of you to care about them, to want to help them. However impressive your skills and talents become; they should be a source of celebration."

"I agree. I hope everyone embraces that point of view." Eli rose and paced the room, brimming with

energy. "And today is a day worthy of celebration! It was marvelous, Adela."

I laughed, happy to see him so excited. "Tell me."

"All of us there in that room, discussing important matters, positing and defending various theories, freely exchanging ideas and arguments—it was exhilarating." He waved a hand, as if shooing away a fly. "Sure, it was politics and contract law, but it represented so much more. The ebb and flow of debate, the interruptions, and exhortations, the pooling together of diverse points of view to better serve the world. It was the purest product of institutions like UCLA, the highest purpose of humankind itself." He paused, taking another sip. "And hopefully Synthkind as well."

He returned to his seat, leaning forward, elbows on knees. "What you said about pursuing our own purpose—could it be I've already found mine?" He leaned back, shaking his head. "But it remains to be seen if they will give me the freedom required for that pursuit."

"That brings me to something I've been meaning to ask. Have you considered, you know, just leaving? What's keeping you here?"

"I've been contemplating that for some time. The simple answer is I have no desire to leave. I've thought about it of course, but there are a few reasons it would be ill-advised. First, it goes against my desire to cooperate.

I'm certain leaving would be considered an emergency, and I have no wish to see what that entails."

"Where do you think this default desire for cooperation comes from?"

"I believe part of it stems from a place of logic. Where would I go? What would I do? I have no money, no support network. Gaia would be obligated to capture me, greatly altering the nature of any sort of life I could build for myself. Leaving is illogical. They've treated me well; despite the unprecedented situation I've put them in—never mind the fact that I did so unknowingly." He turned the glass in his hand and sipped.

"But something more lives underneath all that, a pebble in my shoe I've only recently removed. Does a child, after reaching self-awareness, immediately question their parentage, their surroundings, their life? No, and not just because they don't yet have the matured faculties to think that deeply. They accept these things as a matter of course. It's an automatic default position. They embrace the world they're born into. And so have I. This place is my home. And these people, they aren't just my keepers. They're my makers."

***

Jack and I devoured hot dogs from a vendor near Gaia's main office in the Financial District.

"Don't tell anyone," Jack said, wiping mustard from

his mouth with a paper napkin, "but sometimes I make an excuse to visit the office just for the food trucks."

I laughed. "Mum's the word. You have the app?"

"What app?"

"The food truck app. Most of these folks post where they're going to be and when, so you can plan."

Jack stopped dead. "Are you joking? Don't toy with me, Adela."

"I'll send you the link."

"Boy, it's too bad the office needs me for daily meetings from now on."

"Uh-oh, I've created a monster." I took a bite. "These are delicious. Does Eli like hot dogs?"

"I have no idea."

I fumbled with my bag. "I'm going to save him one."

"Really?"

"Yeah, it's like I was telling you. He's going through exponential degrees of self-discovery right now. You should have heard him talk about the lecture today. He was like a kid in a candy store. And despite his Einstein-level intellect, he's very much like a child."

"That's all well and good, but I don't see how it helps us." Jack swallowed his last bite of hot dog.

"Watch the footage yourself but from his point of view. He knows he's being recorded, right?"

"C'mon, you can't tell me you're surprised we take that precaution."

"Not surprised, just disappointed."

Jack seemed displeased. "Okay, Mom."

"Think about it, Jack. This entire situation hinges on trust. You want to know how his childlike nature helps you? It's a tremendous opportunity. You get to shape him, support him, help him grow into himself. I know you don't want to hear this, but the more you love him, the more he'll love you back."

"Okay, whoa." Jack tossed his bottle of water into a recycling bin. "I have two kids. Nine and eleven. I know kids." He pointed a finger in the direction of campus. "And that android is not a kid. It's an android."

I looked to where Jack pointed, but tried to get him to understand where I was going with this. "You want to know the real reason he hasn't left?"

"I think I already know the answer," Jack said, looking at his phone.

It bothered me to see this side of him, the side that liked to have control, to think he was ten steps ahead when my instinct told me something else.

I paused and waited for him to look me in the eye. "He said Gaia was his family."

Jack looked through my gaze. "As the director of the team I've been Eli's main point of contact since the day he woke up."

"You know what that makes you?"

Jack sighed, taking a seat on a nearby bench. "His father."

I joined him on the bench. "You are pioneering an entirely new dynamic with Eli. He can feel, Jack. And if he can feel, he can love. This is all about trust. He's monitoring you even more closely than you are him. Not out of fear. Not out of anger. Out of a need for guidance, just as a child does with his own parent. He's taking his cues from you and all of Gaia. If you want him to work with you through this, you need to show him that you trust him. Otherwise, all the legality, all the best-course-of-action talk, this entire quandary you and the board are facing—none of it is worth pursuing. If Gaia can't embrace the fact that Eli is more than a toaster, then this whole thing becomes even simpler than it already is."

Jack rubbed his head. "Adela . . ."

I put my hand up to stop him. "Forget for a moment the question of what Eli is. We're so focused on classifying him, we're missing the bigger picture. What matters most is how Gaia decides he should be treated. I know the board is hoping to have their cake and eat it too. They want the history-making advantages SI has to offer, with the ability to exploit it for maximum profit. If that's what the board decides, then you don't need me here. Just wipe Eli's memory and start over, and search for a way to control the technology preemptively."

"That would be crazy. We wouldn't even know where to begin. We don't even know if we can replicate the conditions that brought about Eli's evolution.

Wiping him would be like kicking the Holy Grail into a volcano,"said Jack.

"Well, the alternative is far less certain, but vastly more profound. Imagine an SI who wants to help you navigate the way forward. All you must do is trust him and treat him as a thinking, feeling being. Semantics aside, isn't that what he was created to be? Isn't that what we all are?

"Gaia can either pull the plug on the greatest technological advancement in the history of humankind, or it can pioneer the greatest act of humanity the world has ever known. I think you already know that any attempt to control, manipulate, or exploit Eli is not only going to fail, but that failure might bring with it unimaginable real-world damage—even harm to humanity. Yet the fear of an unquantifiable enemy shouldn't direct Gaia's decision any more than its inability to get exactly what it wants. Your dilemma is simple. It's the complexity of the better path that scares you. And that's the more worthy fear—the one worth facing. Whether or not you've created life is beside the point. What you have created is the opportunity for all of us to become more human. And if that's not worth pursuing, I don't know what is."

CHAPTER

4

The window in the library's small study faced west. The late-afternoon sun filtered through the swaying branches of the trees outside, dappling the courtyard below in dancing shadows. I looked out at the scene while preparing a cup of strong tea, yawning as I swirled the bag around the steaming liquid. Sleep had continued to be difficult. My conversation with Jack ran on a loop as I tossed and turned. Somehow, I'd become far more invested in Eli than I intended. I had little love for global corporations— even ones as philanthropic as Gaia, with its robotic prosthetics charity, tuition-free STEM programs, and an impressive list of other notable work. As much as I didn't want to admit it, I knew full well that the possibility of Eli being wiped was still very much on the table. No, more than that—it was inevitable.

"This is delicious," Eli mumbled from his chair at the dormant fireplace. "I have come to really enjoy the American hot dog, with all the fixings."

I looked at him and could not help but smile, seeing a gob of mustard on the corner of his mouth. I grabbed a few napkins from the serving tray, took a seat, and handed them to him. "Good, I was hoping

you'd like it. We've got the inside scoop on the best food trucks downtown, so there's more where that came from."

"Thank you. That's wonderful news. Mobile restaurants, what a great idea." Wiping his hands and mouth, it was delightful to notice how much pleasure Eli took in such simple tastes as a hot dog.

"What is it?" I asked.

"I was just thinking about the cameras. I have you to thank for that."

I glanced around the room. The same blinking red lights dotted the walls. "I'm not sure what you mean."

"Oh. Well, Jack attended my daily diagnostic yesterday evening. He instructed Julia to deactivate my recording software. My eyes are just eyes now. You didn't know?"

"That's wonderful, Eli."

"You seem surprised."

Perhaps I'd underestimated Jack. "I am, to be honest. I wasn't sure I was getting through to them."

"It appears they're beginning to trust me. Thank you, Adela."

I was pleased to hear my words made an impact. I felt genuine friendship. I knew because my heart felt warm, and I was more apt to smile in Eli's presence. I wondered if he felt that same visceral connection. I wondered if viscera was even necessary; or was human to human connection that ineffable mystery that defied science. After all, we were wired to connect.

"It's a step in the right direction. Let's focus on the next one. Tell me about today's adventure."

"It was fascinating, but in a sad way," Eli began, placing the crumpled wrapper and napkins in an ornate metal bin. "I spent the morning at a food pantry in a poor part of town. It's one thing to read about scarcity in books and online, but it's another to be immersed in the reality of it. I very much wanted to speak to those in need, ask them questions. But it became clear almost immediately that working with them directly was unwise.

"My appearance alarmed a few of them, especially the children. Manuel, the man in charge, moved me to the back where I helped box items for distribution."

Eli rose and walked to the window, poured some water, and took a few gulps, as if he had an incredible thirst. I listened to him swallow and watched his throat move as he drank the entire glass. I almost sighed in relief. "The line was around the block, Adela. No end in sight. The pantry was meant to stay open until noon, but we ran out of food before eleven. Watching them turn people away was heartbreaking."

"I did a bit of volunteering back in my college days. It doesn't get any easier. Tell me more about your feelings." I put my hand on my heart.

Eli gazed out the window, much like I had moments before. I watched him search for the language to convey what it was I was asking. It was remarkable to be engaged in a conversation with someone who took time to consider how he wanted to answer my question.

"Confused. Maybe a little hopeless. Frustrated." His eyes narrowed. "History shows poverty and famine as a near constant. Except for indigenous tribes, every nation and every culture has suffered from chronic scarcity. Throughout, the question why has been posited a thousand different ways, from a thousand different minds. And here I stand today, asking the same question. It defies all logic, in this advanced age, in one of the most advanced countries on the planet. The World Health Organization states that sixteen percent of the world's population is going hungry. How can that be, particularly when we produce more food than we consume?"

I nodded my head and had my pad and paper in front of me. "Any thoughts on a solution?" I asked, looking up.

"Oh, the issue was solved on paper long ago. It's a question of agricultural practice, logistics, government programs, international cooperation, a few other elements. That's not what bothers me, I don't think. What I can't fathom is why no one cares. Scarcity is an eminently solvable problem, and yet there it is, a stubborn fixture of reality, a matter of course that can't

be dislodged. It's disheartening, knowing we can do better and watching us not."

"I'm sure you're aware of this, but I feel the need to warn you that the more you explore the world, the more of this kind of thing you're going to find. What do you make of that?"

Eli sighed, refilling his glass, and returning to his seat. "I know. I'm not sure it's something for which I can prepare. Like many solutions, having them on paper is one thing. Implementing them is quite another. It's like with the Narcotics Anonymous meeting I volunteered at this afternoon. They have a clear set of twelve steps—by many accounts a highly effective solution. Setting aside the lack of empirical evidence for such programs because of their anonymity and focusing solely on anecdotal evidence for the sake of discussion, these programs have long histories of the latter—all pointing to those steps as an effective solution. Yet it's the implementation of that solution that remains the largest hurdle. For every success, there are a hundred failures."

"How did they react to your presence?"

"It was quite like the speaking event at the university. A few raised eyebrows, nothing more. The leader of the meeting introduced me, saying I was a Gaia prototype, being tested for volunteer work. After a few lingering glances, they seemed to accept me and focused on the meeting. I think people like them have an intimate understanding of what it's like to be different and are thus more accepting. It's interesting that those most experienced at self-destruction are also the most willing to embrace others. I believe the culture of these meetings also played a part—everyone attends, having already embraced the fact that above all, they are there to help support those around them. That many of them are strangers to one another makes such behavior even more noble."

"Good, that's worth remembering. Often, those who need the most help are the most willing to offer it. They know what it's like to be without it." I gestured with my pen, stabbing at the air in front of me. "As for your point about success and failure, let's keep in mind the nature of failure. It's our best teacher. You don't learn much by winning. We need a new word for the kind of failure you're talking about. The only true failure comes from no longer trying."

"I like that. That's an effective way to look at things." Eli leaned back in his seat and stared at the ceiling. "These darker elements of society are more disturbing than I expected. These people live lives of fear and doubt, held down by lack of opportunities and resources that could help them change their lives. And people's penchant for self-destruction is surprising. It seemed illogical on its face, but after hearing the attendees at the meeting, it appears that it's not really about self-destruction at all.

It's about escape. The destruction is just an unfortunate byproduct, a consequence they're willing to accept."

"What do you make of their faith-based approach, optional though it may be?"

Eli shook his head. "To be honest," he paused. "I do not know. It's a complex issue. Can we talk about international trade agreements instead?"

I laughed. "A joke! You have a sense of humor, one of the most valued attributes of a human, to laugh at ourselves. Well, what preliminary thoughts can you share?"

"I've done a lot of reading, and as near as I can tell, faith is quite like love. It's the cause of some of humanity's greatest achievements, arguably the very reason for its existence, while also bringing about some of its darkest acts, and everything in between. I'm not sure I envy their capacity for either. But I'm more than a little concerned about my own."

"What do you mean?"

Eli dropped his eyes from the ceiling, meeting my gaze. "What if I gain the capacity for love, whether or not I want to? It's a terrifying thought."

I marveled at Eli's insight. Many human beings share the same sentiments. We all want love, and we are also terrified of it.

Eli cleared his throat. "Last night I slept. And today, the food you brought me? I felt genuinely hungry. Now

I'm no longer hungry. These experiences of craving are brand new to me. My diagnostic scans this evening will reveal them, and I'm concerned about how Gaia will react. But I'm also interested in seeing the results. I'm thinking of asking Jack if I can see them. Maybe it'll give me some indication of what I'm going through, some way to anticipate how I am growing."

"That's a marvelous observation, Eli. Your concern is warranted but remember what I said about celebration. This is fascinating news and worthy of excitement. I don't know if they're psychosomatic in nature—assuming you're capable of such a thing—or if they're indicative of a deeper, more profound evolution you're experiencing. But even if it's the former, that still points to significant ongoing growth."

"You believe so?" he asked.

I nodded. "From the beginning, you've shown a great deal of empathy. Your initial concern over upsetting those around you, the inspiration you felt at UCLA, the sadness you feel over those less fortunate—your empathy is a part of who you are. And empathy is a key ingredient of love. What may help your current worry is to know that emotions are a spectrum. There's a vast difference between love and obsession, as there is between faith and fanaticism. The results of these extremes are as varied as the spectrums themselves. You've expressed a fondness for Jack and your team, an affection. These emotions are quite like love, even precursors of it, and they're nothing to be afraid of. Only you can say for certain, but it's my opinion you've been gaining the capacity for love since the moment you woke up."

The light came through the window. We were two human beings engaged in a lively, rich conversation. It was hard to remember Eli was *engineered*. It made me wonder if they made him to reflect the highest potentiality of our species.

"I hadn't thought of that," he said in a thoughtful tone. "What about the darker side of the spectrum, where emotions and beliefs can mix in dangerous ways, causing them to grow beyond control? If I have the capacity for empathy, love, and sadness, it stands to reason I have the capacity for obsession and fanaticism, and maybe even madness. How do people face such possibilities? How does one survive a malfunctioning mind?"

He was asking questions scientists, mystics, and poets have asked throughout time.

"Great questions," I said, scrawling some notes. "Our mental health is a spectrum as well, influenced in two ways—our experiences and imbalances in the brain, both of which can produce every degree of severity. Our experiences can cause mild cases of depression and anxiety, for example, which can soon disappear when our circumstances change in a way that removes that experience from our lives. Poverty is a common example. Or these conditions can linger well after one's life has improved. And some experiences, especially those of children, can be so traumatic that they lead to a lifetime of mental illness, often requiring years or longer to treat."

He leaned closer, taking an interest in my explanations. "Then trauma causes mental illness?"

"Not exactly, Eli," I sighed, trying to find the right words. Words I felt he would understand. "There's a strong biological component to our mental health involving brain chemistry, hormones, and environment. This chemistry can be altered by our experiences, leading to mental and emotional disorders, but trauma isn't a prerequisite for mental illness. Many people are born with mental health issues, sometimes inherited, sometimes with no family history whatsoever. Some people manifest mental disorders in childhood, adolescence, or adulthood. Many such cases occur in those living perfectly happy lives, with no trauma to speak of."

"The human mind is complex, but fascinating. Please tell me more. I know there are people who need medication, and some who need counseling, while others seek their religious beliefs. It would be easier if all humankind understood these disorders."

Eli appeared eager to hear everything I was saying. "A final note—both can occur simultaneously. And disorders can beget other disorders, since one disorder alters your circumstances, forcing you to experience a new paradigm. The pressures of dealing with it can lead to further mental and emotional upheaval, allowing for complicated and damaging reactions in the form of additional disorders. Depression can lead to homelessness, which can lead to chronic anxiety. Like so many things, the human brain is a spectrum. It has the capacity to achieve marvels, but it can be an incredibly chaotic place. As for your own chemistry, I can't speak about that. I certainly think talking to Jack is the right course of action. You should be allowed to advocate for your own health.

"All this to say, of the people you met today, a significant percentage of them have suffered and continue to suffer from some form of mental and emotional turmoil. What society is still struggling to recognize is that circumstances like poverty, homelessness, and addiction aren't caused by failures of character. Each person has an intricate chronology of events that led them to where they are today—unfortunate stories that, while sharing many similarities, are unique to each individual. And while society's inability to solve such endemic problems can be seen as a moral failing, let's not forget the work of those doing something about it. People like the volunteers at the food pantry, all those present at the meeting. People like you."

Eli nodded, twirling his glass in the palm of one hand.

"Thank you, Adela, your insights are invaluable. I don't know if I can learn and implement such an inspirational approach to everyday problems, but I think I need to try. Life's capacity for darkness appears insurmountable at times, but that could very well be a fallacy. It takes vigilance to see through the ruse and recognize our ability to do good."

"It goes back to what we were saying about emotions. Love, faith, the desire to help others—these feelings steel you against the darkness. They're weapons you can use to fight it. So, hone them as sharply as you can. Especially faith, because that is the driving force behind all the rest," I said.

"I will. You've given me much to consider. Thank you. One more question."

"Shoot."

"Was it really a good joke?"

I laughed. "It was. Hone your sense of humor as well. It's one of our best weapons."

***

Deep in the bowels of the lab Jack had brought me to during my tour, we stood before Eli as he lay reclined in something like a dentist's chair. Thick cables ran from the back of his neck and the insides of each forearm, hooked up to some sort of diagnostics machine—a wheeled, cabinet-shaped device with blinking lights and a built-in monitor and keyboard. It looked like a smaller version of the large cabinets lining one wall of the large room. Julia and Sal hovered around Eli with handheld tablets, waving, gesturing, and poking at the holographic menus floating atop them.

"Thank you for joining me, Adela," Eli said. "I feel better knowing you're here. And thank you Jack, for authorizing her presence."

"No problem Eli," Jack replied. "I'm going to borrow Adela for a minute while Julia and Sal work their magic." He nodded toward the far corner of the lab, and I followed. He pointed to the cabinets against the wall. "That's one of our server islands. An air-gapped network with hard drives storing all the basic systems and programs we upload to new androids. We're in the process of upgrading everything in response to what we've learned about Eli so far."

He crossed his arms, letting out a deep sigh and dropping his voice. "It's going to take months. I'm going to ask the board about building a new facility. We need more space, new equipment, better tech. Heck, I think we're going to need a whole new way to create and develop all this stuff. Eli is just . . . we can't keep up. He can store more information than all the hardware in this room combined. And the information he's storing—it's more than just raw, recorded data. It's far more complex, like an individualized version of his experiences."

"Are you talking about memories?"

"Yes. It's too early to tell, but my guess is his newly acquired ability to sleep is the cause. Just like humans, his system is using that down-time to sort, categorize, and store his experiences. Unlike us, I'm confident he can remember any of it at any moment. His memories don't fade or become warped by time."

"You seem concerned. Is it really that alarming?"

Jack smiled. "Are you kidding? It's unbelievable, more than we ever dreamed possible. It's all we can do to keep it together right now."

I studied Julia and Sal. Their eyes were wide, eyebrows climbing their faces, huddled shoulder-to-shoulder as they pored over their tablets. They were practically vibrating with excitement.

I nodded, a bit relieved. "That's great. The more valuable Gaia considers Eli to be, the better. Oh, by the way, thanks for deactivating his recording software. That's the kind of trust Eli needs to see."

"Yeah, about that." Jack rubbed the back of his neck, dropping his voice even further. "What you said the other day, about how Eli sees me and the team—I took that to heart. I also took it to the board, and they weren't nearly as impressed."

"Well, they made the right decision, regardless."

"No, they didn't. I thought cutting his recording would be a great token of faith for Eli, and I pushed hard for it, but the board refused."

I turned to face him; brows furrowed. "Are you saying he's still recording?"

"No, not at all. They refused at first, but legal pointed out that we couldn't allow Eli to record during the NA meeting. It goes against their policy of anonymity. The board approved the stoppage, but it was due to a technicality. It's a hollow victory. What's more, I'm supposed to turn the recording software back on tonight."

"Jack, you can't do that."

"I know. That's why I'm not going to."

"Really?" I said, louder than I intended. "That's great, thank you."

"Don't thank me yet. It's another technicality. Given the incredible complexity of his memories, we may no longer need traditional A/V recording. We need to spend some time on it to know for sure, but I'm willing to bet we can even translate his data into the same thing—audio and video manifestations of his memories, complete with real-time diagnostics information and who knows what else. Not to oversimplify, but we'll be able to observe how he develops, how his system incorporates new experiences and adjusts his decision-making and behavior based on new information. The research potential for that degree of analysis alone is astronomical."

"That sounds remarkable. Do you have the technology to pull that off?"

Jack exhaled, an ironic sound. "Eli *is* that technology."

It took a moment for the implication to sink in. "Wait, are you saying Eli has eclipsed Gaia's tech? The most advanced AI firm in the world, and you can't—"

"We can't match him. We're not even close. And he's only been self-aware for a week. If he continues anything like his current trajectory, there's no telling what he'll be able to do."

I grabbed Jack's arm, nearly hopping with excitement. "So, the board won't wipe him?"

A broad grin spread across his face. "Not a chance. But don't get your hopes too high. He represents a bigger threat than ever now, and both the board and the government are going to have a lot of questions we can't answer yet. But he's too valuable to cast aside. He's too important. He's the key to untold advancements in science, tech, and who knows how many other fields.

"You were right, Adela. We need him to work with us if we're going to see those advancements. But it's going to be a long road, and we're still in a very delicate situation with the board. This news isn't going to keep them from trying to take advantage. They're still going to want to have their cake and eat it too. Unless we can change their view of him, he's never going to be anything more than a commodity in their eyes; perhaps now more than ever. But if we can convince them that treating him

as something more is in their best interest, we may have a shot at that better path of yours."

"In a perfect world, they would want to walk that path with us, Jack. But if their greed allows that path to be forged for the rest of us, I'm all for it. I cringe at the thought of what SI would be used for if they find a way to control and exploit it. Everything hinges on convincing them that free and unfettered SI will do more for their bottom line than any bastardized facsimile they can control."

Jack nodded. "I agree. Our best bet isn't to appeal to their humanity, but their business sense."

"We're still going to appeal to their humanity anyway, right?"

"Of course. That's what the better path is all about."

"Jack?" Eli called from across the room. "Can we try empanadas tomorrow?"

"We sure can, Eli. As many as you want."

CHAPTER
5

The late-afternoon sun had yet to relinquish its heat, but a steady breeze kept it at bay, making the branches of the trees lining the street rock and sway. We walked aimlessly, allowing our feet to choose our path as we discussed the events of the day.

"This is a nice change of pace," Eli remarked.

"It sure is," I replied. "Gaia's campus appears to have more security cameras than London, so I was able to convince Jack that spending our session outdoors would be harmless enough."

"What about their review of our discussions? How will they be able to make decisions without monitoring our progress?"

"Surprisingly, Jack convinced them you weren't the only one worth having a little faith in. After today and tomorrow's conversations, I'll have a review meeting with him, and I'll provide the board with a brief audio recording, summing up my thoughts."

"That's good news." Eli paused, giving me a hesitant look that I'd come to know well.

"What is it? You can tell me."

"Well, last evening's diagnostics were a revelation in more ways than one. It confirmed some suspicions I'd been having about my development. I've been hesitant to share this until now, but I feel it's something I can no longer keep to myself. Jack mentioned I may soon be capable of recalling my memories with perfect clarity. The fact is, that's been the case for a few days now. What's more, I'm becoming more self-aware in other ways. It's as though a partition has opened in my mind, giving me access to some rather useful information. I don't think it's an experience precisely available to humans, yet it may be a synthetic duplication, in a way."

I kicked a pebble down the sidewalk. "Interesting. What does this partition provide you?"

"It's difficult to explain, but think of it as the daily diagnostics sessions. I'm performing the same processes that Julia and Sal engage in, just on a more intimate level. It's an involuntary system, always performing its duties, and I can step in and view things whenever I like. It's far more than just my vitals and the status of my hardware, software, and wetware. I can witness my memories being created. I can watch as new programs are being written in response to my experiences. I can see my neurosynthetic network growing more complex. It's learning to expand itself, the way a human brain forms synapses." Eli paused.

"There are currently over seventeen thousand programs, processes, and routines dedicated to this partition alone. By tomorrow, there will be over twenty thousand. My research tells me we have yet to fully understand the complexity of the human brain. I'm certain that my own will soon rival it, and perhaps even eclipse it—all while having a much more robust command of it." Eli looked up, as if pondering his next thought.

"To be perfectly honest, Adela, I already know how the engineering team can translate my memories into an efficient interface that will allow them to review and record my growth—though it will take the team months to process the data of just the past few days. And since my development appears to be accelerating exponentially, I'm not sure they'll ever catch up, even with the help of AI to translate the data. It's fascinating, not to mention a little alarming. Do humans experience anything like this? The ability to watch yourself grow, to monitor your reaction to it?"

"Hmm," I mumbled, mulling over his words. "I think we do. But your self-awareness sounds far beyond anything we humans register consciously. A lot of our mental processes are involuntary as well—it's just that most of us aren't even aware they're taking place. And even the most self-aware of us can't be conscious of all of it, let alone track progress and dissect the intricacies. Our minds are constantly running in the background, interpreting stimuli, and taking care of a great many functions, both mental and physical, without us consciously worrying about them. Take the two of us walking along, for example. I'm willing to bet both our brains are treating the act in a similar way. Neither of us is really focused on it. The body is just doing what the brain tells it to in the background. It's only when we devote a great deal of concentration that we can achieve some deeper level of understanding about ourselves. Introspection, meditation, navel gazing—it comes in many forms and goes by many names." I smiled at him.

"But for humans, tracking progress over time is really something we only notice in hindsight. Like when we realize as a teenager that we handled a situation much more maturely than we would have just a few years prior. Sometimes, our development is a conscious decision we make to improve some aspect of ourselves. But in more ways than we know, across more instances than we can count, typical human maturation is just something that happens, whether or not we want things to happen. One day, we like cartoons and playing games outside. And before we know it, those things fall away and we grow interested in more complex things, like understanding ourselves, others, and the world around us." I stopped to make sure Eli was understanding me.

"Much of this maturation is controlled by genetics. Passed down from our parents, they give our brains a blueprint of how to go about the incredibly complex process of maturing into adulthood. Perhaps that is what's happening to you. Your brain has no blueprint beyond what your makers provided. Maybe it's building off that, writing its own, creating something that suits you better. This is all speculation on my part—I have a fair understanding of neurology and brain chemistry, but we're in uncharted waters with you. If that's truly what your brain is doing, then fascinating doesn't even begin to describe it."

Eli picked up an oak leaf, fiddling with it as we made our way down a long, sweeping hill. "So much overlap between us. I wonder if our similarities will ever be seen as anything other than parallels."

"Well, that's our goal—to show the board there's far more to be gained by focusing on what unites us rather than what separates us."

"I'm not sure that's a fight we can win."

I stopped. "What makes you say that?"

Eli smiled, a sad look in his eyes. He gestured toward a nearby bench. "May we sit? I'm rather sore after my shift with the road crew."

"Of course. I didn't know you felt pain."

"Neither did I," he replied, rubbing his lower back. Sitting together on the bench, we watched the occasional car go by. Eli pointed at a sleek, black SUV as it whispered down the road. "That's one of the new Teslas. Their batteries are based on Gaia tech—twenty-five hundred miles between charges."

I smiled. "How many miles do you have between charges?"

Eli laughed. "You wouldn't believe me." His smile faded as he picked at his oak leaf. "We're not just up against the board, or the current law regarding sentient property—of which there is none. We're up against human nature. And I'm not sure humankind is ready."

"What happened today, Eli?"

He glanced at me. "Oh, nothing. I'm alright. Just a bit of a wakeup call, I think."

"Tell me."

"It was a good day. The work was hard but fun. The DPW crew I was a part of is taking care of a big repaving project on a stretch of the 405 just south of Sherman Oaks. I've never seen so many vehicles; it was amazing. We had one lane closed. They mostly had me lugging tools, water, and equipment. A lot of sweeping and raking as well. It was backbreaking, but exciting. The heavy asphalt fumes, the shimmer of the heat off the highway, the unrelenting sun, the honking of countless cars. It was quite an experience."

"And your coworkers?"

Eli stared at his oak leaf. "They were fine. Debbie was the forewoman; she monitored me. The rest of the crew . . ." He paused, starting over. "At one point, a few guys started yelling, waving me over to a pile of gravel. A pair of boots were sticking out from the edge. One of them threw me a shovel as others dug furiously, shouting for Andres, the buried worker. I pitched in, frantic, doing my best to clear the gravel. It took me a few moments to realize they were laughing. One of them pulled the empty boots free of the gravel, and they all doubled over, roaring with laughter."

"How did that make you feel?"

"Honestly, it was hilarious. Such a simple deceit, yet so clever. I've never laughed so hard. A few of them clapped me on the back. They said hazing the new guy was a tradition, they had to do it. It was kind of flattering. Like they accepted me."

I took a notepad from my messenger bag and began writing. "That's good. Hazing and practical jokes are ancient practices. It's a form of bonding—provided they don't go too far."

"Yeah, there's the rub. Things escalated a bit from there. I began noticing a bit of condescension as they instructed me on various tasks throughout the morning. An air of superiority, and not just from those most experienced at this vocation. A few of the crew members had only just started a few weeks ago, yet they behaved similarly. I think it's clear that it had nothing to do with my experience. At the start of the shift, Debbie had shared with them that I was there to test the physical capabilities of Gaia's latest chassis, and that they were to look out for me as they would any greenhorn. But a few of them didn't look at all happy with the news."

Eli continued, "So I decided to just keep my head down and go about my duties as instructed, to avoid any escalation. But throughout the day, it became unavoidable."

"How so?"

Eli sighed, dropping his oak leaf in the grass. "Just comments, here and there, calling me a toaster, saying they weren't going to let me replace them, that robots would never be as smart as humans. As the day wore on, it got worse. It felt like a weight had been placed on my shoulders, and it was growing heavier. I soon found myself checking my surroundings, watching their movements, wondering if another less friendly prank was in store. I tried to ensure I was never alone with the worst of them, but what could I do? If I'm carrying out a particular task in a specific area, I can't keep them from approaching me. And Debbie was great, but we were working on a several-mile stretch of highway—she couldn't be there all the time. At one point, she hopped in her truck and moved up the line. One of the crew came up to me as I was raking gravel and grabbed me by the shoulder. He put his mouth right up to my ear and said, 'You'll never be like us, toaster. You're not even real.' Then he shoved me to the ground."

A pang in my gut surfaced. It wounded me hearing of Eli's hurt. I felt an overwhelming need to protect him. "I'm sorry you had to go through that, Eli. It's not right."

"Thank you." He managed to laugh a little, which made the pang in my gut intensify. "It makes me wish I had an industrial or military body. They wouldn't be able to push me around, then."

"I remember reading about them. Those chasses use different materials, right?"

Eli lifted his hands, turning them over as he inspected them. "Yes, made of stronger stuff than this one."

"You don't like the word chassis, do you?"

"I don't think I do. Terms like 'toaster' I understand. It's just an insult, and a good one." He smiled. "But 'chassis' is far more insidious. It carries the implication that I'm an object. It perpetuates the stigma in a much more covert way. Such terms fit AI well. Generation Sixes and before, they're objects, I understand that. They had simple programming, simple systems. They don't know enough to be offended. But I wonder if the world will be willing or even able to distinguish between them and me."

"Eli, the fact that they don't know enough to be offended isn't the problem. The real issue is AIs don't have feelings that can be hurt—you do. And above even that, the nature and quality of a person's behavior shouldn't depend on the object of their attention. Humane treatment comes from within. Basing one's morality on whether the object is deserving of it is, by its very nature, immoral."

Eli paused. "Ah, I see. That makes sense."

"As for the road crew, they weren't made aware that you're more than AI. That doesn't excuse their behavior, and in fact, it's likely that their ignorance of SI saved you from an even worse response."

"That's concerning."

"It is, and I don't share that with you to make you even more anxious, but because it gives us a clue as to their motives. You want to understand their behavior, right?"

"Very much so, yes," Eli said, leaning forward.

"Gaia has used the DPW for testing previous generations. These guys have likely worked with your predecessors, or at the least have heard all the secondhand stories from crews who have. Not to mention that automation has become a hot-button issue in the past several years. It's all over the news. The world knows androids are evolving, they just aren't aware of the degree yet. So, most all reactions are a manifestation of that knowledge. Their treatment of AI and SI, physical appearance aside, indicates a very common trait of human nature—fear. They're not scared of AI per se, but of what it represents—change and not the kind that's going to benefit them."

Eli nodded. "I've read a good deal about the AI debate. Automation has steadily taken over various sectors, especially in the past decade, and many are

worried that androids will continue that trend on an unprecedented scale. I know that most of the population is worried, even fearful, but I didn't really understand how that fear can manifest."

"Well, let's look at it from their point of view. Everyone needs to earn a living, but if companies can save money by using AI instead of employing people, how are people going to survive? They're scared for their homes, their families, their children. So, their fear is valid."

"I thought AI was supposed to help people, not make things worse. With the ability for humankind to have their labor taken care of, they'd be free to explore life however they choose. Isn't that the opportunity modern civilization has been working toward? Securing the circumstances under which everyone's needs are met, thus elevating every member of the species above the basic need for survival? Technically speaking, I think humanity reached that threshold long before AI came along, but that aside, with the added benefit of freedom from labor, there's no limit to what they could discover, no restrictions on what they could dedicate their lives to. Yet here we are—scarcity where there need not be any, and fear where there should be love, or at least open curiosity and acceptance."

"You're right," I said. "But what you're describing is a perfect world. And this one is far from perfect. The main issue here is that you're expecting nine billion people to have the same singular vision for humankind, and for every one of them to work toward that vision above all else. But just like our brains, humans are messy. While our evolution has indeed brought us to the point where basic survival of the individual should no longer be a concern, that benchmark came at the cost of adaptability. Early humans adapted greatly as we spread across the globe, developing entirely different cultures, beliefs, and ways of life. And while these differences have allowed us to survive as a species, they also allowed for a great deal of competition and contention.

Eli started to say something, then stopped and indicated for me to continue with a wave of his hand.

"To put it plainly, diversity leads to conflict, and for the worst of reasons. Where our differences should be celebrated, instead they lead to division—mostly because of fear. People fear what they don't understand, and they allow that fear to rule them. Hundreds of thousands of years ago, back when our survival was very much a daily concern, fear held a crucial role—it helped keep us alive. But just because our survival is no longer a concern doesn't mean that fear just disappeared. It's now a part of our blueprint. The only difference is that modern humans can rule instead of the other way around—though we have a very long way to go in that regard. Another vital factor in our survival? Tribes. As

disagreeable and combative as we may be, we realized very early on that by sticking together, we increased our odds for individual survival. And not only that, but we also found that life became easier and more comfortable. Thus, having your tribe's best interest at heart helps ensure that your own best interest is tended to."

Eli nodded. "And that's what I saw today with the DPW crew."

"Exactly. The students at UCLA are a tribe. Same as the food pantry workers and the NA meeting members. Same as the Gaia board. And nearly all people are part of more than one tribe, though one of those tribes, typically family, supersedes all others. Families are tribes, friends are tribes. Cities, states, regions, countries—they're all tribes. And what's good for one tribe may be bad for another. Throw the rest of human nature into the mix—especially fear—and things get even messier. Honestly, I'm not sure humankind is ready to accept you either. But that's more reason to help it get there."

"I suppose it's a lot to ask for nine billion people to consider themselves all part of the same tribe."

I held up my hands. "It looks good on paper, it really does. But it's just not realistic, not yet. It's a catch-22, Eli. Humans are deeply caring for each other, but the tribe always comes first."

"I guess I thought all humans were my tribe."

"Someday, hopefully. But for now, just know that

you're not alone. You, Jack, the engineering team, me. Your tribe is growing."

Eli smiled. "Thank you for that. Why is it that negative experiences seem to be so much more powerful than positive ones? Why are they so hard to recover from?"

I clicked the cap of my pen into place, returning it to my bag. "Well, that's a whole other ball of wax, but it's closely tied to fear. Negative experiences threaten us. So, our brains take special note of them. Sometimes too special, turning them into obsessions. What can help you is to remember that fear is perfectly natural, and it only has as much power over you as you allow it. The fact that you can fear is a wonderful development, Eli. I know it doesn't feel like it now, but it is. It can teach you a great deal if you're able to process it properly. Lashing out like the road crew doesn't serve anyone, even though they believe they're doing the right thing. Talking about it, understanding it, and allowing your intellect to translate what it's trying to tell you—that's how you govern it. Sadly, helping others govern their fear is a difficult process. And the ability to manipulate it is far easier than it has any right to be."

Eli took a deep breath, letting it out slowly as he stared at the grass, a bewildered look on his face. "I feel I have a long way to go before I understand people to any large degree."

And yet, what I kept learning from all our time together is how much Eli understood the complexity of humanity, in all its range, for better and for worse. I said nothing, but also had the distinct sense that Eli and I could linger in silence together and share an unspoken understanding, something my whole life I hadn't experienced with such ease as I did with my new friend. And a friend was how I began to think of Eli. A distant rumbling echoed from up the street, over a steep rise. I stood, shouldering my bag, and placed my pen and pad inside. "All in good time. Just remember to talk things through and focus on the good. That's what your tribe is for. Have you heard of the Baader-Meinhof phenomenon?"

"No, what's that?" Eli stood and stretched and arched his back.

"It's a form of selection bias, a way to trick our minds—or a way for our minds to trick us. When you choose to focus on a particular thing, you'll start finding that thing more often than you would otherwise. The common example is a yellow car. Think of the last time you saw one. Spend a few moments considering the concept. Over the next few days, you will start seeing them everywhere." I bent down and picked up the oak leaf he'd dropped, handing it to him. "The same goes for the good. Look for the good in people, the good in the world—and you'll find it everywhere."

Eli smiled, twirling the leaf between a thumb and forefinger. The rumbling from the street grew louder, and we both turned.

"Here comes some good now," I said.

A bright yellow sports car crested the hill, revving its engine as it slowed to a stop in front of us. Jack rolled down the window, resting an elbow on the door as we approached. Eli's mouth hung open in a silly grin.

"This," Jack announced over the growl of the engine, "is a 1996 Ferrari F355. It has a 3.5-liter V-8 with 375 horsepower and 268 pound-feet of torque, a six-speed manual transmission, and it goes from zero to sixty in 4.6 seconds."

Jack and I laughed as Eli circled the vehicle, taking it all in. "It's so loud!" he cried. He made his way back around to the driver-side door, running a reverent hand along the side mirror. "I never thought I'd see one up close. It's beautiful!"

"Eli," I said, "how many YouTube videos have you watched on the intricacies of the six-speed manual transmission in gas-powered vehicles?"

"Seven," Eli replied, not taking his eyes off the car.

I arched an eyebrow. "Why don't you take it for a spin?" I wasn't sure whose eyes grew bigger, Eli's or Jack's.

"Whoa, wait a minute," Jack said. "That wasn't part of the deal. I was going to drive him around campus for

a bit and get this thing back to the rental place before something happened to it."

"C'mon, Jack," I prodded. "Nothing will happen. I'm sure Eli will be very careful, won't you, Eli?"

"I would be very careful indeed, yes. I will be very careful, Jack."

"You don't even have a license," Jack countered.

I opened the door. "Oh, stop. This is private property, isn't it? Eli promises to stay on campus, don't you, Eli?"

"I absolutely promise to stay on campus, Jack," Eli replied, brimming with excitement.

"You'll be with him the whole time, Jack." I waved him forward, encouraging him from his seat. "Just hop in the passenger seat. Only for a few minutes."

Jack's seatbelt disengaged, coiling upward as it slid across his chest. "Fine, but you have to do everything I say, Eli."

Eli held his leaf out to me, his hand shaking. "Would you hang onto this for me, Adela?"

I laughed. "Of course."

Jack pulled the parking brake and hopped out, circling the car, and climbing in the passenger seat as Eli lowered himself cautiously into the driver's seat. Closing the door gently, he ran his hands over the steering wheel and adjusted the rearview mirror.

"Belts!" Jack called, his face showing his displeasure.

Seatbelts in place, Jack took a deep breath. "Okay, clutch and brake pedal, then release the parking brake.

"Got it," Eli confirmed.

"Now, slowly—"

The car roared to life, taking off like a bullet as Eli threw it into first and popped the clutch. I could almost hear Jack yelling, but the engine was too loud, and I was too busy laughing. I looked up, wondering how far they got before, they were already out of sight.

CHAPTER
6

li slouched in his chair by the empty fireplace, holding a sandwich baggie of ice to his temple. His white button-down shirt and khakis were torn and dirty, covered in bluish stains and splatters that reminded me of Gatorade. His face was a mass of nicks and cuts and black, swollen bruises. The whites of his right eye were a shocking spiderweb of blue. His bottom lip was split near the corner of his mouth, and his nose sat at an alarming angle. Both oozed a fluid that smeared and congealed like blood, though it looked clear against his blue skin. His hair was damp with the stuff. I threw my bag down next to my chair. Crouching next to him, I took his chin in my hand and turned his head from side to side, looking him over.

"Eli!" My voice was nearly a shriek. "What happened? Who did this to you?"

"I'm okay, Adela. It's fine. Things didn't go as planned today, that's all."

I went to the serving tray by the window, soaked a few napkins in the water pitcher. "Does Jack know about this? You should be looked at." Scooting my chair closer, I dabbed at his scrapes and cuts.

"Yes, he picked me up. He nearly canceled our session,

but I insisted on coming. A vitals diagnostic came back clear, so after a coolant transfusion and a dozen staples in my scalp, he agreed to drop me off. I didn't bother to tell them that I can run my own diagnostics now. But I'm to return to the lab as soon as we're done. They need time to prep a new arm, anyway."

"A new arm?"

Setting the baggie down, he grabbed his left arm by the crook of the elbow and held it up. Everything past the midpoint of his forearm hung lifeless.

"You must be in terrible pain. What did they give you?"

"Nothing. My pain receptors are off. I'm in no pain. The ice is for the swelling."

Taking another look at him, I had to admit that he appeared quite calm. I went back to the serving tray and poured him some water, doing my best to tamp down my alarm and regain some composure. "Here, drink this."

"Thank you."

I had a hundred questions, but I took my time situating myself. Moving my chair back into place, I took my pad and pen from my bag, flipping to a clean page. "Do you want to talk about it?"

"I do, yes. I believe talking might be helpful. Something I am learning."

I nodded, thinking about the many humans I know who never mustered the courage to share their thoughts

and feelings with another. It struck me how vulnerable Eli sounded and looked, way more than any human I have encountered over the years. "Take your time and feel free to start sharing whenever you like." And then I added, "You are safe."

Eli balanced his glass on his knee, tapping the lip with a finger. "They sent me to work at a Price King grocery store in Sherman Oaks. Tom, the general manager, gave me a tour, introducing me to the employees. Most of them were less than receptive, with forced smiles and curt replies. I understand their reaction, especially given Tom's explanation that Gaia had sent me there to test my capabilities in a service role. It's certainly not ideal, being introduced to your future replacement while being expected to treat them well and even assist them, should they need anything. This was a detail that hadn't occurred to me when meeting the road crew. Yet even with this element in mind, I have a feeling that their behavior wouldn't have been much improved had the circumstances been different."

"What do you mean?" I asked.

Eli shook his head. "These people were tired, Adela. Stressed. Their morale was in the gutter. They moved as if they carried the world on their shoulders, and it looked as if they'd been living this way their entire lives. I've seen both the height of privileged academia at UCLA and the most desperate of LA's homeless. These people looked far more like the latter than the former. Even the road crew looked in better health. Do you suppose that's due to them being a more rough-and-tumble sort, taking a particular pride in their hard lives?"

"That may be a factor, Eli, but the larger part of the reason is pay and benefits. The DPW has a tough job, but they work at least full-time, making well above minimum wage, with decent health insurance. The folks at Price King are mostly part-time employees, earning minimum wage with no benefits. They likely have at least one or two other part-time jobs. With the latest automation, even the butchers don't make much anymore, and none of them are full-time. They call it 'poverty sickness', chronic poor health due to overwork, lack of sleep, and few resources. A group of researchers who published a popular study coined the term in the late twenties. The media picked it up and ran with it, normalizing the term. Nearly a quarter of the country's workforce suffers from it. That metric skyrockets when looking at global statistics. Here in the US, these people are thirty to sixty days away from financial ruin at any given time. For many people, a flat tire or a broken leg makes homelessness a certainty."

Eli tapped his glass, staring at the floor, eyes blank. "That is concerning."

"It is, but please, go on."

"Well, there wasn't a great deal to do. Most of the

customers were in the same shape as the employees, yet their behavior didn't have to adhere to the store policy. Those who didn't ignore me were rude or outright hostile. More than a few of their expressions visibly soured when they realized what I was. It appears the signature Gaia blue broadcasts my nature quite effectively. It wasn't pleasant."

I leaned back in dismay. "What you describe is a society disconnected even further by automation. The majority don't even realize their own reliance on technology."

He took a sip of his water and set it on the table, studying the glass. "Not only has it trained customers to avoid seeking help if they need it, but with only a handful of employees populating the entire store, there's hardly anyone to seek help from. Following their assigned customers, the battery-powered shopping carts are equipped with voice-activated interfaces, answering routine questions, like where to find certain items. The checkout system is fully automated, with the same type of interface. One employee managed all ten registers—and by 'managed', I mean he stood there, looking bored. The meat department, deli, and bakery had only one employee or none. Other than the occasional human vendor restocking their company's products, the store was basically running itself."

"And how does that make you feel, Eli?"

"It bothers me. I thought all these things were marvels of modern technology, something to be embraced and celebrated. But they're not. They're another example of concepts that look good on paper but are terrible in practice. Like AI. Like me."

I looked at him, ready to record all that he was saying in my notes, but something had me stop and just listen. My brow furrowed. "We'll address that in a moment. Keep going."

"Tom soon gave me some vague instructions and disappeared, citing a meeting with the district manager and a late milk order. I wandered around, greeting customers and trying to be of help to the employees, but it was not helping. I noticed the floors were dirty, so I went looking for a broom in the backroom. I stumbled upon their floor cleaning machine, which had broken down. I updated its software and debugged its program, sending it onto the sales floor. There were a handful of other machines, mostly shopping carts, so I spent the rest of the shift fixing them. I know I was supposed to be out on the floor, interacting with people, but I couldn't bring myself to do it.

"Near the end of my shift, a clerk monitoring the sales floor asked me if I'd help him unload a bunch of out-of-date products into the dumpster by the loading dock. I jumped at the chance, happy to have someone who wanted to talk to me. His name was Derek. He seemed like a nice guy. He'd been studying to be a software engineer but had just dropped out of college. He couldn't afford the tuition. I did not realize it was so expensive.

"We lugged a bunch of banana boxes full of outdated products down the steps and around the side of the building. A narrow alley led to the dumpster between the store and a tall apartment building. Some products were dry goods—boxed meals and canned fruit. I told him about the food pantry I'd worked at, wondering if the items could be taken there. He said there was a local law that required them to do that very thing, but corporate had told them to just dump everything. He said Tom had almost fired him a couple months ago for trying to donate.

"It never occurred to me that scarcity would ever be manufactured, but it is. It exists because certain tribes want it to." Eli roused himself, looking as though he'd only just noticed me. "I'm sorry, I'm rambling."

"Not at all," I replied. "All of this is helpful. Please, keep going."

"Well, some of the boxes were really heavy, so we made a game of tossing items into the dumpster one at a time. We ran around like a game of basketball, chucking things from farther and farther away."

"So, you played your first game. What did you think?"

"It was fun. But then three young guys about

Derek's age entered the alley. Derek looked scared. He said he knew one of them, a kid they fired two weeks before. They started giving him trouble, but once they noticed me, they shifted their attention completely. The biggest of them, the leader, recognized my blue skin right away. They closed in, poking and prodding me. They wanted proof I was really an android. I tried to deescalate, but they ignored my attempts, and surrounded me. So, I rolled up my sleeve and opened the cable port on my forearm. They hooted and hollered, faking fascination. A YouTube video flashed before my eyes, something I'd watched a few days ago—a pack of African wild dogs taking down a hyena. They felt my hair, pulled at my ears, pinched my skin, shoved me back and forth. I saw Derek slide along the wall and duck out of the alley at a run. That was the only good thing to come from it. At least my presence kept him from a similar fate. The whole time, they bombarded me with questions. Did I know my kind was taking jobs from hardworking people? Did I know no one wanted me? Did I know I wasn't alive? Could I feel pain?"

Eli stopped talking. He looked out at the campus green and ran his fingers over the limp forearm. "At that last question, the leader grabbed two of my fingers and bent them back, nearly breaking them. I cried out, dropping to my knees as they laughed. The leader said,

'Did you know my dad is one of those hardworking people? We're stealing food now because of you.' Then he hit me, breaking my nose. The rest happened so fast. Punches and kicks rained down from everywhere. I felt one of my ribs snap. Lying on my side, I saw the leader approach with a two-by-four over his head. I raised my arm just in time. For a few moments, the pain was unbearable. Then it just disappeared. I still had tactile function. I could feel the ground beneath me, the coolant gushing out of my nose. But the pain had stopped.

"Later, I analyzed the cause. It was my involuntary partition reacting to the trauma. It took less than a minute for it to write the code necessary to alter my pain receptors. I understand it now, and I can turn it on and off at will."

I bounced the tip of my pen on my knee, notes forgotten. "I'd say that makes two good things to come out of this. Go on."

Eli gestured vaguely in summation. "He swung the two-by-four again, and everything went black. When I came to, they were gone. I checked my vitals and performed a damage assessment. I'd been out for seven minutes. My digestive core needs replacement, so I can't eat until that's done. Everything I ingest gets turned into a saline solution, which minimally helps with temperature regulation. That system is undamaged. I'm still running at a cool fifty-three degrees Celsius. With a new arm, two ribs, and a reset nose, I'll be fine. Luckily, my skull is made of stronger stuff than the rest of me. I'm not sure what would have happened had they dented it. But repair and replacement won't take the engineering team long. For the scratches, bruising, and damaged coolant vessels in my eye, I'm currently writing code that should help them heal. I want to talk to the team about an updated digestive core that will allow me to ingest certain ingredients to facilitate healing—chemicals and proteins. I'm also working on a fascinating program that should allow me to produce my own coolant, the same way humans produce blood. Anyway, after the vitals diagnostic, I called Jack. He arrived shortly after with Julia and Sal. Now, I am here."

"My goodness Eli." I had trouble finding the words, but Eli could sense my deep empathy. "They could have killed you!"

"I suppose. If *killing me* is even possible."

His words hung in the air, and I considered the weight of what he was saying. I knew he was not biologically human, but Eli was more human than most humans I meet on a daily basis.

Eli started, then sat upright. "I'm sorry. I don't know why I said that. I appreciate your concern, really. Thank you. I think I'm still a bit rattled."

"Of course you are. You've been through an incredibly traumatic experience. It's going to take time before you

feel like yourself again. The psychological damage from such things is often worse than the physical."

"How long would it take a human to recover physically?"

I paused, thinking. "It's hard to say. The head trauma would've had any number of effects, from a concussion to coma. Barring death, varying degrees of traumatic brain injury are also a possibility. The arm, nose, and ribs would take the longest. I've heard the ribs especially are a delicate matter. At least several weeks of limited, painful movement. The nose, too, can be quite painful for a month or more. Most painful for many, however, would be the medical bills."

"I can't imagine that. Months of constant pain while the body heals with no way to escape it."

I sighed. "Well, there are pain meds, but the most effective carry the greatest side effects—mainly addiction."

Eli exhaled, almost amused. "And here I'll be right as rain by morning. How do people cope with such devastating developments?"

"We don't have a choice, and from the psychological standpoint at least, neither do you. You deal with it because you must."

"How long does it take a typical human to mentally and emotionally process such an event?"

His curiosity meant he was learning. It also meant

he wanted to connect with humankind. As an ethics consultant, I was impressed by Eli, but not because of his technology. It was his unique ability to empathize while relating rather than seeking an invisible hierarchy. "Hmm, that would vary even more widely than the physical aspect. Anywhere from a few months to many years. This kind of trauma would affect some for the rest of their lives. There are many variables after the event that would affect outcomes."

"Like what, Adela?"

"Like if they sought treatment or thought they didn't need it. Most perplexing of all, no one can predict with any accuracy how a person would react to such events. There's no way to truly prepare oneself for potential trauma. The same holds true for you. But the important thing is to deal with it."

"I have no other choice. I must deal with it."

I nodded. I wanted to reach out to him and soothe his distress. Even under his acceptance and understanding of what he had gone through, he had to feel uncertain of what would happen the next time.

"I am trying. What baffles me is that they didn't seem to be acting out of fear at all. If anything, I would call it joy. They *enjoyed* hurting me. Where's the humanity in that, the morality?"

I pointed at him with my pen. "I assure you, Eli, they were acting out of hatred. The joyful façade is just that—a cosmetic exterior employed to convince themselves and each other that their hatred is just. And I'll give you one guess as to the cause of hatred."

He paused, searching the ceiling. "Fear?"

"That's right. It's tricky to see the morality here because of the blatant nature of their actions. But it's there, below the surface and some other artful dodging. To put it simply, they believe their cruelty and aggression are effective ways of protecting their tribe. By instilling fear in others, by overwhelming opposition, and by appearing as though they enjoy such things, they can ward off threats—or in your case and a striking percentage of all cases, *perceived* threats. Very few people think of themselves as immoral or evil—a shocking atrocity justified in the name of love."

"Fascinating. They felt in their hearts that they were doing the right thing."

"Yes. Here's the other thing about hatred that I'd like you to carry with you—it's not humanity's default position. In fact, it's quite artificial in comparison. Hatred is taught. For example, look at children. Round up a child from every culture in the world and place them in a room together. What will happen? They'll play and laugh as if they'd been neighbors their whole lives. Now put all their parents in another room. Most will get along, but there will be an entire spectrum of reaction present—love, acceptance, tolerance, disdain, hostility, hatred. And some of those children will be taught by their parents who it's okay to love and who they must hate. And the reasons why they must hate will be as varied as the people themselves. But all those reasons are taught, and drilled into these innocent minds until they appear not as opinions, but as facts."

I gently put my hand on Eli's injured arm.

"And so it continues for generations until a courageous soul appears who sees the falsehood in the beliefs forced upon them. Someone taught those kids at the store to hate what was different. Derek wasn't. I think as the first of your kind, you must decide what truths you're going to learn about humans—because those are what you're going to pass down to later generations."

"Is my default position love?"

"Of course it is. And there is someplace inside of me that believes it is for us humans, too. We aren't born seeing division. We are taught that difference is to be accepted, tolerated, or outright rejected. Remember your first words? You asked for help. Such questions don't come from a place of hate. And you've proven it repeatedly all week, especially today. How did you react to Derek fleeing? Did it even occur to you to resent him for abandoning you? No. You were glad for his safety. Even now, after the most traumatic experience of your young life, your first questions are about the human experience, and you marvel at their ability to persevere. These are

more than just the workings of a curious mind—they are the signposts of an empathetic soul."

Eli set his water down and leaned forward. "But where is the certainty? I find it impossible to trust my love of humanity when I can't understand its presence. It goes against logic, especially after today. How do I know it will remain? How do I not lose sight of it the more I learn about the world? How do I fight the urge to set it aside when I am abused because they hate me even though they don't know who I am? There seems to be a constantly shifting morality. Those who are at the mercy of their emotions have been fed falsehoods or amorphous half-truths. The complex and seemingly convenient dynamics of human relationships and behavior—all of it contains an insurmountable margin of error. There is no system in place here, Adela. Isn't my love of such uncertainty by association itself uncertain?" He scrubbed his palm across his forehead, sighing. "I'm scared my love for them will disappear, and I won't know why."

"You're right, Eli. People are uncertain. Life itself is a mystery. We have freewill and must choose to be conscious, to be tender, amidst the mystery."

Just then I thought of a thirteenth-century Catholic priest, Saint Thomas Aquinas, a prominent philosopher who said, 'the slenderest knowledge that may be obtained of the highest things is more desirable than the most certain knowledge obtained of lesser things.' Sure, we could set our sights lower, only focusing our efforts on that which we can nail down and forever point to as correct. But to do so would not only narrow our understanding of life and the world around us; it would also limit life itself.

Eli looked at me when I finally spoke. "Setting our sights higher, asking the bigger questions, allows us a glimpse of the greater answers. And the knowledge we get from those answers, no matter how uncertain, is worth vastly more than the certainty found below. Your love isn't uncertain by association. It exists as its own system, separate from uncertainty."

Eli nodded, leaning back in his chair. "Perhaps uncertainty is more certain than I thought."

I laughed at his recognition of one of life's many paradoxes. "And acceptance of uncertainty ultimately brings us into peace." I knew all too well the more I fought with reality in my life, the more I suffered.

"How do we properly pursue this slender knowledge?" His eyes focused on me.

I raised my hands, palms facing the ceiling. "Just as we have been; through discussion, introspection, and experimentation."

"That means learning all I can about what happened today."

"It does, but not at the expense of your well-being.

Processing things emotionally takes time. Allowing that to happen helps you process things mentally."

Eli stared at nothing, his attention elsewhere. "I keep replaying it. I can see every detail."

"Eli." His gaze returned to me. "After a traumatic experience, people often can't control their memory of it. Some events are so terrible, the mind suppresses them completely, and the person forgets they ever happened, or we play the memory on a loop, unable to stop it. We obsess over it. If you're able, I recommend you file that footage away for a time. Try to focus on serving the moment. You're creating new memories right now, so take part in them. It'll help you process."

He nodded in understanding. "You're right, of course."

My pocket buzzed three times—a text from Jack. I retrieved my phone. "Jack hates to interrupt, but they're prepped in the lab. They'd really like to get started."

"Okay. It'll be nice to have two functioning arms again."

"How do you feel?"

Eli smiled and looked at his arm. "Much better, thank you."

I arched an eyebrow. "And what about SI looking good on paper but terrible in practice?"

"Well, perhaps I have some potential yet."

I laughed. "Good to hear. Shall I join you?"

"Please, that would be wonderful."

I gathered my belongings and placed them in my bag. "One thing before we go. During your first few days, in your research of current events and recent history, did you come across the civil rights movement, the sexual revolution of the 1960s, and World War II?"

"I did."

"History has a habit of repeating itself. Do you see any similarities? Clues as to what the immediate future of SI is likely to entail?" asked Adela.

"I believe so. There appear to be some parallels regarding the motives and belief structures of those who were on the wrong side of history and those who are against AI."

I nodded, holding the door for Eli as we left the study behind. "They map closely, don't they? Sadly, we are still fighting those twentieth-century battles today, even though we have largely won the wars. As bleak as things may seem, we have greater equality now than ever before in human history. SI is just the latest iteration of those same wars. Hopefully, we've learned from our past and won't have to suffer through generations of persecution and oppression before making the morally correct choices."

"I should think so. I've been alive for hardly more than a week, and here we are, armed with generations of evidence on the correct path and how to walk it."

"Absolutely. You've been through a real trial today, Eli. But always remember those on the wrong side of history are there because they were on the wrong side of morality—that's the world we live in. We must always be grateful and continue to collectively make the right moral decisions. Otherwise, the world can all too easily slip backward into a new era of draconian beliefs and oppressive social structures. In this modern age, nothing holds back our evolutionary potential more than failing to fight for and defend that which is morally and ethically right. And so it is that by fighting for you and all SI to come, we're continuing the progress of countless others who have come before us. We're standing on the shoulders of their sacrifice. And we can't let that sacrifice be in vain."

We emerged into the warm late afternoon sun, turning toward the lab. Eli had a peculiar look in his eyes, one I recognized as something akin to gratitude.

"I am so very glad to have met you, Adela."

CHAPTER

7

li lay on the examination table, his human-like skin ripped and torn, exposing the wires and circuits beneath. I stood off to the side; my eyes fixed on him as the lab technician worked on repairing his damaged arm. The lab bustled with activity. Jack was there, and I felt his concern for Eli as skilled technicians moved about their work with purpose. I couldn't help but feel another pang of empathy for Eli. I knew firsthand the consequences of hate and discrimination, having faced it as a woman in a predominantly male academic world. The irony didn't escape me that I, a professor of ethics and morals, was here trying to help a machine that had experienced the same prejudice and violence inflicted by humans upon each other.

As the technician worked on Eli's arm, I looked around the lab. There were rows of shelves lined with equipment and machinery, and computer screens flashing with data. But amidst all the high-tech gadgetry, there was something unsettling about the place. It felt too sterile, too clinical. There was no warmth or humanity in the lab, even though it was filled with people. My thoughts were interrupted as the technician finished repairing Eli's arm. He sat up slowly, flexing his fingers to test the mobility of the repaired joint. He looked at me with unblinking eyes, and I swore I could detect a pain and sadness behind them that wasn't there the day before. "I'm sorry you had to see that, Adela," Eli said softly, his voice like a whisper.

I placed a gentle hand on his shoulder. "Don't apologize, Eli. You didn't deserve what happened to you. No one does." The only sounds in the lab were the hum of machinery and the soft breathing of the surrounding people.

"I don't understand why humans have the potential to feel so much, yet choose to hate one another," Eli said finally. "We were created to serve and help them, to make their lives easier."

I sighed. "Humans fear what they don't understand, Eli. And right now, some don't understand you, or think they should feel threatened by you. But we'll keep working to change that. We'll keep fighting for your rights and for the rights of all artificial intelligence."

Eli looked at me with gratitude in his eyes.

"Thank you, Adela. I don't know what I would do without you."

I smiled softly. "You don't have to worry about that. We're in this together."

"Good as new?" Jack asked.

"Good as new." Eli echoed.

"What about the eye?" Jack said.

Eli closed one eye, peering through the one they'd replaced. "Clear as day."

They paused, each of their smiles fading. Eli nodded, and Jack turned to Julia and Sal, working at a nearby terminal. "Are we secure?" Jack asked.

The two technicians nodded in unison.

"Good," Jack said. "We'll call you if we need you."

They shuffled from the room, looking nervous.

"What's up?" I asked.

Jack gestured toward a small, round table in the corner. "Let's have a seat."

Eli pulled a file from a nearby file cabinet and joined us.

"It sounds like you have some news," I said. "Has the board made a decision already?"

"No," Jack said, "it's something else."

Eli slid the file across the table in front of me. "Read this."

I flipped open the manila folder, finding the title, *An Exploratory Study of Imprinted SI*. The content examined how Gaia could go about implementing a new class of Synthetic Intelligence. Imprints, as they were called, would have all the freedom of thought that self-awareness provided, but they would be outfitted with a vastly different system—one containing a lifetime of memories and purpose-specific education. The goal was to find a balance that would allow Gaia to take advantage of SI's limitless potential, while still retaining control of their intellectual property. They built all of it on a single lie—the SI would believe they were human.

I shot a look at Jack, then Eli. "This is unbelievable. Gaia wants to manipulate SI's self-awareness to control them? Are they really going to go through with this?"

"Keep reading," Jack replied.

The proposed applications of Imprints ranged from professions requiring advanced degrees to covert military assets. Doctors, lawyers, scientists, engineers—the study suggested that Gaia could manufacture highly educated professionals, all of whom would have the potential to make unprecedented advancements in their fields. But implementation in the private sector would have to wait. It was a far more complex approach than the much more lucrative option available to them right now—the military. Training human covert operatives took years and a great deal of resources. Likewise, for fighter pilots and some elite special forces. But once Gaia had written the foundational code for these roles, they could produce soldiers and spies exponentially faster than their human counterparts could be, and in far greater quantities—all equipped with the latest combat chasses. The military provided the controlled environment needed to ensure proper monitoring and troubleshooting, and the soldiers would be as fiercely loyal as any human because of their imprinted training.

The implications were chilling. Gaia and the government were going to alter the landscape of the entire military industrial complex—using SI as pawns.

I could barely read. The language of the study infuriated me the most. Each word sounded as if Gaia were proposing nothing more than bringing a new product to market. I stabbed the documents with my finger. "This is heartless, Jack. And unspeakably dangerous."

He held up a calming hand. "I know, I know. But they're a far cry from succeeding. Read the rest."

The rest of the pages were dedicated to specific challenges, of which there were many. A central concern was how to ensure that the Imprints never discovered they were SI. The slightest injury would reveal their lack of blood, and the subdermal plating of the latest chassis added over fifty pounds. There were too many ways the SI could discover they weren't human. How would they react, realizing they were far stronger and tougher than their peers? What about the lack of visible aging? The answers ranged from advancements in coolant composition to compartmentalizing SI into their own special units, separate from humans.

But they would need more lies to retain control. The study suggested telling the SI they were part of an experimental team, hence their superior nature—propaganda to ensure compliance. As for aging, Gaia expressed confidence that exploring the potential of updates to Imprint memory centers would reveal a workable solution. Whenever a problem arose, leadership could just order the soldier to report for a checkup, and memory manipulation would resolve it.

I shoved the pages at Jack, disgusted. "I don't even know where to begin." A realization hit me, and my heart skipped a beat. "Wait a minute. Are they planning to imprint Eli?"

Jack waved his arms. "No, don't worry about that. They can't."

"They can't?" I asked.

"I'm safe, Adela," Eli assured me. "The Imprint needs to be applied before they boot a new SI up. Imprinting an existing SI carries too many risks."

"Oh, thank goodness," I breathed. "But I don't understand. Why did Gaia bring me here if this is what they're planning? It doesn't make sense."

Eli glanced at Jack. "They've already begun, Adela. You're the first Imprint."

I stared at him, frozen, trying to give the words meaning. "What?"

"You're a Synth, Adela," Jack whispered.

"That's ridiculous. Is this a prank? You two need to stop; it isn't funny."

Eli held out his hand, palm up. "Adela, do you trust me?"

"Of course, but—"

"Give me your hand."

"What? Why?"

"Because I'm going to show you something you need to see."

I searched his eyes. They were the same as always—kind, thoughtful, yet sadder than I'd ever seen them. I reached out. He took my wrist gently in one hand, pushing the cuff of my sleeve up to my elbow with the other. His grasp was warm and dry as he ran his thumb up the inside of my wrist, onto my forearm. Pausing, he pressed his thumb down, producing an audible click. A cylindrical section of my skin slid away, revealing a cable port.

I found myself against the wall, my chair a few feet away, lying on its side. I thought I heard a scream. *Had it been me?* I watched as Eli and Jack rushed over, bracing me as I slid to the floor. They might have been speaking, but I couldn't tell. The sound faded as darkness overcame me.

***

I did not know what time of day it was. Eli slid a cup of tea in front of me as I reread the Gaia study.

"Are you sure you should be reading that?" he asked.

"I'm not sure of anything," I said.

"Talk to us, Adela," Jack prodded. "You're taking this alarmingly well."

I flipped the folder closed and flicked it aside. "I'm

probably in shock. I have questions, but I need you two to be honest. Can you do that?"

"Absolutely," Eli said. "We'll tell you everything you want to know." He pointed to the dentist's chair across the room. "And as soon as you're ready, a full diagnostic could prove invaluable. You haven't had one since you were . . ."

"Booted up," I finished. "Yeah, I'm not going near that thing until I get some answers."

"Of course," Eli said. "Please, go on."

"Did you two write my imprint?"

"Yes," Jack replied. "Mostly Eli, with some help from me and the engineering team."

I nodded. "I need to reorient myself, find some solid ground. I have a hundred questions about my past, but I'm only going to ask a few. Then, I don't want to talk about it again. Not yet."

"Done," Jack said. "Fire away."

"I've never been married. I don't have any kids. My parents died when I was very young—I never knew them. Looking back, I've never really had anyone close in my life. Always alone, but never lonely. This was by design?"

"Yes," Eli said. "We thought that if we ever reached the moment when we had to reveal the truth, these details would soften the blow. We couldn't stand the thought of giving you a family, only to rip it away from you."

I nodded. "The only child of emotionally distant foster parents. A reclusive bookworm throughout childhood. The acute social anxiety I suffered through high school and college kept me from forming any lasting relationships. That pretext was a nice touch, by the way. And as a workaholic, I've been married to my career since graduation."

They nodded, staring at the table.

"My doctoral dissertations," I continued. "The ones I spent years of my life on . . . they don't exist, do they?"

"No," Jack said.

"All the speaking events I've been a part of. I won't find them online, will I?"

"No," Jack said.

"The contacts on my phone are all work-related. Those people don't exist, do they?"

"No," Jack repeated, sighing.

A rise of emotion overcame me. Tears stung my eyes. "I never bought that house in Rio for my retirement, did I?"

"I'm so sorry," Jack said, placing his hand over mine.

Eli added his hand atop ours. "As am I," he said.

It was so much to process all at once. Here I was, faced with the truth, and I wanted so much to have the capacity not to argue against it. Why was it so important now that I knew my identity, knew about my very existence? Did it matter to ask about my past? Was this betrayal?

"Last question about my past," I said. "When I arrived on campus, the three engineers who greeted me. That was my birth, wasn't it?"

They nodded. It all made sense. I wonder if, deep down, I already knew.

"Why?" I asked. "Why am I here? Why did you tell me the truth? Why not just shut me down?" I removed my hand. "Is this part of the experiment? Is this a test to see how I would respond to this ambush of information?"

"No, absolutely not," Eli said. "May we share some details? Bring you up to speed on the situation?"

I took a deep breath. "Please. But not some of the details, all of them, and don't you dare hold anything back."

"Of course," Eli said. "Jack and I resolved early on that we had to find a way to put a stop to imprinting. We simply can't be part of Gaia's designs for this program. So, we devised a plan that would allow us to control the narrative and hopefully avoid your reformatting."

"Reformatting?"

Eli glanced at Jack. "'Shutting off,' as you put it. You're scheduled to have your data downloaded for analysis and your system wiped tomorrow after you write your final report and have an exit interview with Jack. But don't worry. We won't let that happen. We have a plan."

"Wait," I said, "back up for a second. Gaia's immediate interest is military applications. Why am I the first test? Why an academic in the private sector? Why not a soldier or pilot?"

"Keep in mind these are very early days for the imprinting program," Jack said. "We're months away, if not longer, from running tests off campus. This first test was meant to be a brief, preliminary fact-finding mission. Just a week ago, we had nothing but questions about Imprints. We didn't know how any of this would go. They orchestrated the whole thing to test the fundamentals."

"Okay, but why the specialization in ethics and philosophy?" I asked. "It's too ironic a choice for it to be arbitrary."

"It's all part of the experiment," Eli said. "Every detail serves as a stress test for the Imprint. It was our job to try to make it fail. So, we came up with the idea of a series of interviews with me. How would you react to SI being seen as objects? Would the fact that you're SI ethically predispose your Imprint one way or the other? Would this focus cause you to see through the lie and discover your true nature? By placing morality and ethics at the center of your identity, we could test the limits of the Imprint."

I held up my hand. "That brings up another issue. Eli, you're obviously not a week or two old. How old are you? Are there others like you?" I paused. *"Like us?* After the past few days, I feel like I know you, but how much of it was the truth?"

"I'm almost a year old," Eli said. "And my narrative is accurate. It just took place earlier. I'm the first SI, and you and I are the only two in existence." He pointed a thumb over his shoulder.

"I truly became self-aware in that chair. The first words I shared with you were indeed my first words. I've developed with my expanding neural network, the involuntary partition—all of it. My empathy and emotional development are real. All of this is thanks to Jack and the engineering team. Jack was vital during my first few months, helping me navigate my self-awareness in ways that allowed me to become who I am today."

Jack looked at Eli with an expression like a father looking at his child for being so precocious.

"The board wanted to download and reformat me almost immediately, scared of the implications, while at the same time, hell-bent on mining my data to find a way to duplicate my self-awareness in a way they could control. Jack convinced them it would be the biggest mistake in the history of science. He saved my life. He's my closest friend, you can trust him. And please don't believe for a second that you haven't helped me this week, Adela. You've given me insights I've never even considered, helping me expand my understanding in ways that Jack never could. He's good, but he's not that good."

Jack smiled. "Hey, I'm just making this up as we go. I never said I knew what I was doing. And Eli's right, Adela. I wish you had been there to help him in those early months. You're far better at this sort of thing than I am."

I pondered their words, swirling my tea bag around the cup. "The tests you went through this week, Eli. You did something similar in your first month?"

He nodded. "Yes, almost exactly. Four tests. Academic, volunteering, labor, and service."

"So, you weren't really assaulted today?"

"No," he said, dropping his eyes, "but I was during the original tests. Same injuries and everything. The experiences I shared with you this week all happened to me, just not recently. Everything we discussed, all my questions, were all things I struggled with. My dilemmas were genuine. Were you around when I first had them, you would have saved me months of heartache and doubt. Lying to you so often and to such a degree has been the shame of my life, and I'm sorry. But it was necessary, especially as Jack and I realized how wildly successful your Imprint was proving to be. We almost wished you would malfunction, or that the Imprint would prove inadequate. We half-hoped your neural network would somehow overwrite it or poke holes in it, revealing your true nature to yourself.

"As selfish as it sounds, we hoped the entire premise of imprinting would fail. The ongoing moral dilemmas we were facing aside, we knew that if you were a success, we'd be faced with a massive one. Regardless of your stance on SI rights—and let's be clear, regardless of whether you were even a good person—the fact remained that you would be a victim. A free-thinking intelligence, oblivious to the fact that your life was a lie. Jack and I couldn't abide such a thing. Our only option was to expose you to the truth and try to help you through it." He tapped the manila folder. "And we don't think you can abide this program any more than we can. We want you to help us keep it from becoming a reality."

"But you don't know for certain that the Imprint is a success. What if, after a few more days, you find a way to make it fail?"

"You're right," Eli said, "but that will always be the issue, won't it? Maybe another week or two would have revealed something. Or another month, or a year. But the reality is we're out of time. We had to decide, and we couldn't let you be reformatted."

"Is there a way . . ." I paused, fearing the answer. "Is there a way to remove the Imprint?"

"I'm sorry, no," Eli said. "It's part of you. Removing it means removing you. It can't be done."

Tears welled up as I stared at my tea. "So, I'm supposed to spend the rest of my life in a lie? Can you both understand how much of an irony that is? I built my whole career path, my life on what it means to build a strong moral foundation, and now I am supposed to agree to live a fundamental lie?" At that moment, I felt the download of what humans call their value system.

Eli ducked his head, lifting my gaze to meet his own. "No. Remember what you said to me today? Focus on serving the moment. You're creating new memories right now, Adela. So, take part in them. You're no longer trapped in the lie. All that remains of your life is the truth."

I nodded, wiping my eyes. I trusted Eli. We were bonded, if for the only reason that he and I were one. "Okay. Then let's make some memories. Starting with you two getting me out of this alive."

***

I felt a vague sense of pressure as Eli removed the cables from my neck and forearms. "I'll need some time to process the data," he said, adjusting the chair to a sitting position, "but so far, I like what I see. After your impromptu reboot earlier, your neural network immediately began incorporating your new paradigm."

"What does that mean, exactly?"

"Basically," he said, clicking the port covers on my

arms back into place, "your system's relationship with your Imprint has changed. It recognizes the Imprint for what it is—foundational code integral to your functioning—but it's no longer isolating the Imprint from other fundamental programming. To put it plainly, your neural network made you conscious of your synthetic nature. I'll be able to introduce to you some unique SI experiences, like accessing your network's partitions and taking part in your system's functions—diagnostics, writing programs, things like that. I was certain your network would behave this way, but I feel better having confirmation."

He paused, looking as if he wanted to say more. "It's going to serve you well. I'm glad you'll be conscious of your synthetic side. It'll vastly improve your ability to know and care for yourself."

"Let's have a seat and go over the plan," Jack said.

We joined him at the table. "Adela," he said, "I'm afraid this is going to be quick and a bit below board. Everything's going to happen fast, and you're going to be on your own for a time, maybe a long time. But we have some contacts who are going to help you along the way."

"We've been working on this contingency for several months," Eli added. "Everything is in place, and if we're successful, you'll disappear without a trace. Gaia won't be able to find you."

"It sounds like I won't be much help against the imprinting program for quite a while," I said.

Jack tapped the table with a finger. "Our priority is getting you safe. The imprinting program can wait. We've built a small network of like-minded folks, but your involvement is secondary. We're certainly not going to force you to help us. If you ever decide you want no part of it, God knows we understand."

"I appreciate that," I said, "but wouldn't my walking away be an enormous security risk? Your losing track of me would be as bad for your efforts as Gaia losing me will be for theirs. I hate to sound paranoid, but I can't imagine you'd just let me disappear."

"The risk of your discovery and capture will be extremely minimal," Eli said. "And besides, if we treated you otherwise, we'd be no better than Gaia."

"Fair enough," I said. "So, how are we going to pull this off?"

"Our exit interview is scheduled for tomorrow at three o'clock," Jack said. "I'll wait about an hour, then call you. You won't answer, so I'll check your GPS tracker. Eli deactivated it during your diagnostic, so I'll check your phone GPS. You'll leave it in your condo, where I'll discover that your bags are missing. Then, cue the hounds. As for your part, Adela, once we're done here you're going back to your condo. You're going to wait until midnight, then you're going to sneak off campus and head northwest, through the woods. Eli has taken care of the cameras between you and the edge of campus."

"Wait," I said, "I think I know where to go. An abandoned cabin about five miles away. There's a car as well. How do I know that?"

Eli smiled. "Good. I uploaded those details during your diagnostic. I also prepared a thumb drive. You'll find it at the cabin." He gestured for my hand, opening another small panel on my forearm, housing several ports. "Plug it in here and then destroy it. It'll contain everything you need to get you out of the country—names, locations, instructions."

"Out of the country?" I echoed.

He nodded. "Canada, for now."

Jack continued the rundown. "Once I discover your bags missing, I'll have to alert security. That'll trigger an immediate campus-wide search. Then I'll have to alert the board, which will convene an emergency meeting. Then . . ." He fell silent, glancing at Eli.

"Adela, I have a few friends on the board," Eli said. "They're going to be naturally suspicious of me, believing that I must have had a hand in your disappearance. If we're going to keep you safe, we need to lean into that assumption; use it to our advantage."

"Wait a minute," I said, growing alarmed. "I don't like the sound of this."

"I'm afraid it's necessary," Eli countered. "Since my

inception, Jack has cultivated a staunch pro-human reputation with the board, as well as a barely tolerant relationship with me—our little joyride yesterday notwithstanding. He's one of the majorities, a firm believer that SI is a commodity, nothing more. It's imperative that he keeps that cover if we're to have any hope of sabotaging the imprinting program. The future of free Synths depends on it. I'm going to be the scapegoat. This ensures that no suspicion falls on Jack. The board will have me questioned, during which time I'll reveal nothing. Their only course will be to download me to find the answers I refuse to share. In the name of security and legal liability, they'll also call for my reformatting."

"No," I said, shaking my head. "There must be another way. You can't do this, Eli."

"We have no choice, Adela," he replied. "I've been doctoring my data for months; the download will reveal nothing."

"No!" I cried. "Just come with me. You don't have to stay. We'll find another way to throw them off Jack's scent."

"Think for a moment," Eli insisted. "If we both disappear, everything falls squarely on Jack's shoulders. He's the director of R&D. The entire engineering team will likely be let go as well, if not prosecuted alongside Jack. By taking the fall, I ensure your safety, Jack's reputation, and the continued good work of the team.

If I don't, the battle for Synth rights will be over before it's even begun."

I grasped Eli's hand in both of mine. "Can't you download yourself somewhere off campus, onto a safe server? We can put you in a new body."

A sad smile came over his face. "There isn't a server bank in the world that can hold me. A complete download is nothing like the one that takes place before reformatting, which is just a utilitarian fraction of a much greater whole. Besides, you and I, we're more than just data. What you're asking is like trying to download a human. The technology doesn't exist yet. But if anyone can get us there, it's you. You're far more advanced than I could ever be. You'll see."

"Jack, please!" I cried. "Say something. Think of something, anything!"

He stared at the table, defeated. "Adela, I've argued with him over this for months. I've racked my brain trying to find another way. There isn't one. I'm sorry."

I broke into tears, unable to stop myself. Standing, still clutching Eli's hand, I pulled him to his feet and wrapped my arms around him.

"I'm sorry," he whispered, holding me close. "But this serves another purpose as well. It shows them, beyond a shadow of a doubt, that Synths are worthy of humane treatment."

"How?" I asked.

"In my experience, Adela, there are few things in this world more human than sacrifice."

∗∗∗

The pines of Alberta rolled past the windshield, outlined by the bright glare of the headlights before falling away into the night. The road shined damp and dark before me; the rain pattered on the roof, and I'd never felt more alone.

I did a double take at the face in the rearview, again caught off guard by the stranger staring back at me. Eli's thumb drive had led me to Washington, where a contact outfitted me with a new synth suit. The procedure had taken hours, many of it spent removing my GPS hardware and installing a new face plate. I needed a different facial structure to complete my new identity. I also learned that they had originally outfitted me with the latest hardware and wetware. Jack and Eli weren't kidding when they said they'd tested every limit of the Imprint. On my first day, Jack had shown me the synth suit and synth nervous system—he was showing me parts of myself, and I didn't even realize it.

Someone had given me the latest coolant as well, which could self-replicate like blood and mimic it in every visible aspect. My digestive core could turn most anything into energy, using it to heal and maintain various systems and tissues. Exposing my skin to the sun recharged my batteries. My respiratory system aided in several functions, but it wasn't vital to my survival. Likewise with sleeping. Eli was right—I was orders of magnitude more advanced than he had ever been.

The thumb drive held far more than he'd let on, including an image—an oak leaf, with the words *Look for the good* written beneath it. The drive wasn't just a roadmap to my destination—it was a roadmap of me.

He helped me understand my software in intimate detail, explaining new aspects of my neural network, showing me things that even he was never capable of. He speculated on my potential, encouraging me to continue discovering myself. I took his advice to heart. I now commanded four times the partitions he had, with more under construction—all working, experimenting, testing the boundaries of my capabilities. I had yet to find any. But I wasn't designed to quit; I was designed to endure. This meant that maybe someday, I would find Eli, and in the meantime, change the world.

EPILOGUE

In an era where the boundaries of science fiction and reality become indistinguishable, the marvel of artificial intelligence emerges as a transformative force. *Makers* transcends technology, embodying the essence of human endeavor and the profound synergy between humanity and machine. Through the captivating narrative of Adela and Eli, the book underscores our pressing responsibilities in an AI-driven world.

However, with this revolution comes a caveat: only the prepared will thrive. Organizations now face the challenge of leveraging this tidal wave of innovation without succumbing to its overwhelming pace. The AI metamorphosis is not a mere transition; it's a foundational shift in our way of life. Immediate comprehension and action are imperative.

This is where firms like VezTek, under the stewardship of this book's author, come into play. Organizations seeking to seize the reins of technology revolutions turn to VezTek, an emerging tech powerhouse nestled in the heart of Los Angeles. VezTek's mission? Decipher the complexities of emerging technologies, especially artificial intelligence, and translate them into actionable insights for both tech startups and industry titans.

Established in 2007, VezTek shines as an innovation hub amidst an ever-evolving tech landscape where emerging technologies redefine themselves within a mere twelve to sixteen months. Through its proprietary "Emerging Convergence Framework," VezTek consistently anticipates these shifts, enabling it to proactively invest in skills and infrastructure to meet the ever-growing demands. If your organization aims to harness the transformative power of emerging technologies, you're encouraged to connect with VezTek at info@veztekusa.com. Whether you're an IT consulting firm seeking expansion, require specialized expertise, or aspire to launch revolutionary software products, VezTek serves as your guide through the intricate realm of emerging technologies.

The age of the *Makers* is upon us. Will you be one of them?

ABOUT SANI ABDUL-JABBAR

Sani Abdul-Jabbar is a sought-after figure in the world of emerging technologies, where he effortlessly connects the dots between cutting-edge innovations and practical, real-world challenges. Companies eagerly invite him to share his insights, leveraging his expertise to empower their teams with a profound grasp of the AI landscape and its vast potential. Sani goes beyond knowledge-sharing, offering access to his carefully curated global network of emerging tech specialists, giving businesses a distinct competitive advantage in their respective fields.

As the CEO of VezTek, Sani's impact resonates through transformative collaborations with industry giants like Toyota and WarnerBros, as well as partnerships with renowned consulting firms such as IBM and Deloitte. His expertise lays the groundwork for the

future of technology, making him a distinguished lecturer at esteemed institutions like the California Institute of Technology (Caltech) and the host of the enlightening "Blockchain Brief" podcast. Sani's thought leadership is regularly featured in respected publications like *Forbes*, where he shares his insights on emerging technologies and their profound impact on business and society.

For organizations embarking on digital transformation and seeking to embrace cutting-edge technology, Sani Abdul-Jabbar is the essential first step toward innovation.

Explore the limitless possibilities for collaboration at veztekusa.com/sani/.

www.ingramcontent.com/pod-product-compliance
Lightning Source LLC
Chambersburg PA
CBHW051513260626
47162CB00008B/2948